EVER
READY

The Broken Spear Endorsements

What a privilege to have the opportunity to be one of the first to read *The Broken Spear: Reformation Rising*, the first in a new series by the award-winning author Ruth Ann Ellinger. Historical fiction with a base in true history and family ties is some of my favorite books to read and from the first page, the reader is engrossed in the familial relationships and ties and potential adventure and strife that lay ahead. Ellinger is a gifted author of intrigue and drama.

MARIE A. GILMORE

Editor and Publisher of the award-winning *Osprey Observer* and *Christian Voice Monthly* newspapers. Gilmore is a published author of *Open for Business! Now What?*, a non-fiction small business book. She speaks locally to small businesses and organizations.

The Broken Spear by Ruth Ann Ellinger sheds a bright light on the complexities of the Scottish Reformation and its effect on the clans and people of Scotland. History comes alive through her characters' struggles to make sense of the intrigues surrounding the Scottish court and the possible catastrophic effects those intrigues might have on Clan Carmichael. Faith and loyalty are tested and sacrifices must be made for the good of the country, the church, and most especially, for family. A fine read for fans of historical fiction set in Scotland.

CAROL UMBERGER

Author of *The Scottish Crown Series: Circle of Honor, The Price of Freedom, The Mark of Salvation*, and *The Promise of Peace*

EVER READY

Reformation Reckoning

RUTH ANN ELLINGER

Ambassador International
GREENVILLE, SOUTH CAROLINA & BELFAST, NORTHERN IRELAND
www.ambassador-international.com

Ever Ready: Reformation Reckoning
©2024 by Ruth Ann Ellinger
All rights reserved

ISBN: 978-1-64960-628-0
eISBN: 978-1-64960-677-8
Library of Congress Control Number: 2024940984

Cover design by Karen Slayne
Interior typesetting by Dentelle Design

Scripture taken from the King James Version of the Bible. Public Domain.

This book is a fictional dramatization based on actual events and was drawn from a variety of sources. Any names, characters, and incidents not based on historical events are all products of the author's imagination or are used for fictional purposes. Any resemblance to actual events or persons, living or dead, is entirely coincidental. Any mentioned brand names, places, and trademarks remain the property of their respective owners, bear no association with the author or the publisher, and are used for fictional purposes only.

AMBASSADOR INTERNATIONAL
Emerald House
411 University Ridge, Suite B14
Greenville, SC 29601, USA
www.ambassador-international.com

AMBASSADOR BOOKS
The Mount
2 Woodstock Link
Belfast, BT6 8DD, Northern Ireland, UK
www.ambassadormedia.co.uk

The colophon is a trademark of Ambassador, a Christian publishing company.

To James

The courage to let go and start again is true courage.

Acknowledgments

I WISH TO THANK ALL those who helped with furthering this story by their valuable insight, offering ways to improve every facet of this project.

I wish to thank my editor, Adele Brinkley, who has assisted me over the difficult places in the manuscript and been my editor and friend throughout the years.

Thanks to my husband, who long-suffers with me through the ups and downs of the writing process, encouraging me when I feel overwhelmed with such a daunting venture into such epic history. He is my constant reassurance.

Thanks to my publisher, Ambassador International—the editors, project managers, and staff who have helped in publishing and promoting my books these many years. Thank you all, and God bless you.

Finally, I thank Jesus, my Lord and Savior, the One Who inspires me, believes in me, and loves me. "Thanks be unto God for his unspeakable gift" (2 Cor. 9:15).

Note to My Readers

IN THE *STONE OF DESTINY* series, which takes place during sixteenth century Scotland in the early days of the Protestant Reformation, I have written a tale of tragedy and triumph, heroism and bravery. Using historical facts, I fictionalize my Carmichael ancestors' involvement in the remarkable events of that day.

Some have asked why I write historical fiction with such daunting research and detail. The adage says, "Those who do not learn from history are doomed to repeat it." So how do we learn from history? By writing it down. We record the important events of our time on paper. If we rely solely on memory, we will probably forget those things that, at times, have altered the course of the world. Scripture teaches us in Isaiah 30:8, "Now go, write it before them in a table, and note it in a book, that it may be for the time to come for ever and ever." For this reason, I write about the past events from a biblical perspective that we may learn from history.

It is best said in the words of Matthew Henry:

> The prophet must not only preach this, but he must . . . *write it in a tablet*, to be hung up and exposed to public view; he must carefully *note it*, not in loose papers which might be lost or torn, but *in a book*, to be preserved for posterity . . . *for a standing testimony* against this wicked generation; let

it remain not only to the succeeding ages, but forever and ever, while the world stands . . . so . . . the scriptures . . . shall continue, and be read, to the end of time. Let it be written . . . To shame the men of the present age, who would not hear and heed it when it was spoken. Let it be written that it may not be lost; their children may profit from it.[1]

So, I write.

—Ruth Ann Ellinger, Author

---

1   Mathew Henry, "Doom of Incorrigible Sinners (720 B.C.)," in *Isaiah 30, Matthew Henry's Commentary on the Whole Bible*, Accessed April 24, 2024,   https://www.biblestudytools.com/commentaries/matthew-henry-complete/isaiah/30.html.

Chapter 1

Lanarkshire, Scotland

May 1539

They were stoned, they were sawn asunder, were tempted, were slain
with the sword: they wandered about in sheepskins and goatskins;
being destitute, afflicted, tormented.

Hebrews 11:37

"BURN THE LYING HERETIC!" SHRIEKED a bent and twisted old crone standing near the execution pyre, where stacks of rain-drenched wood encircled a tall stake jutting upward from the center. She held a wooden crucifix in her gnarled hand. From beneath a tattered, old shawl, she extended a scrawny arm toward the bishop presiding over the chaotic scene.

The execution site sat next to the outer stone wall that surrounded Saint Andrews Castle. The castle housed the wealthy and powerful bishops of Saint Andrews, the ecclesiastical center for Scotland. It perched majestically atop a rocky promontory adjoining the North Sea in the ancient kingdom of Fife. Rain, wind, and saltwater beat relentlessly at the stone foundation, slowly eating away at the granite stonework.

The royal guard dragged the neglected-looking prisoner from the depths of the despised bottle dungeon, a pit shaped like a bottle, dug into a corner of the interior castle walls. The condemned man stood before a sour-looking bishop with a barrel chest and large hawk-like nose that bent slightly to the left—evidence of some previous mishap.

The prisoner struggled to stand. Wavering unsteadily, he leaned against a guardsman for support. The cleric chosen to preside over the execution glanced around nervously at the prisoner and then at the waiting crowd. He wanted to get this miserable business over. He was uncomfortable with this assignment, incensed over being chosen for such an unpleasant task.

A crowd of onlookers milled about, stamping their feet to keep them warm. A steady drizzle of chilling rain swept in from the cold North Sea, turning the narrow roadway into a muddy mess of slippery cobbles. The perverse old crone's irritating voice joined the ever-increasing cries of the eager crowd awaiting the nod from the presiding bishop, a signal for the fire to be lit.

Through the densely packed mob, a pathway was cleared by the royal guard, their swords at the ready. They slashed their weapons perilously close to the restless throng causing the swarm of onlookers to fall back. A space was opened for the prisoner, who was dragged before the bishop. The prisoner's hands were tied in front of him, his head bare, his face bruised and swollen. Deprived of food, cold and emaciated, he could barely stand.

Several bedraggled-looking men charged with setting fire to the pyre, struggled to keep the torch burning as the cold rain continued to fall. The torch sizzled and hissed until at length, a steady flame was met with cheers from the crowd.

But before the prisoner was placed onto the pyre, one of the uniformed royal guardsmen rode forward on his mount, grabbed the unsuspecting prisoner, and threw him across his saddle. The guard swiftly thundered away on a well-muscled, nondescript Galloway pony. Speeding away from the castle wall, he left the remaining royal guard and the bishop speechless.

What had happened? Had Archbishop Beaton pardoned the prisoner at the last moment, thereby showing himself to be merciful as the newly appointed cardinal for the pope of Rome? If so, the council in charge of the execution proceedings had not been informed. Perhaps the family of the prisoner had offered a bribe to the archbishop. It was not uncommon to buy a stay of execution if the monetary amount was valuable enough.

Their swords drawn to control the angry rain-drenched crowd, the remaining royal guardsmen, several of whom were mounted, hastily conferred with the bewildered bishop presiding over the execution. Then the head guardsman galloped away to consult with David Beaton, archbishop of Saint Andrews, who had judged the prisoner a heretic, a traitor worthy of death.

The royal guardsman returned quickly and informed the archbishop that a man impersonating an on-duty officer made off with the condemned heretic, rescuing him from certain death. Immediately, the entire garrison was summoned and ordered by the furious Archbishop Beaton to pursue the prisoner and his rescuer. When found, both would be burned without an opportunity for mercy.

After freeing the condemned man from certain death in this daring rescue attempt, William Carmichael arrived wet and weary at the designated safe house. The location was hidden by an ancient wisteria vine that enveloped a private close, gated and secured with chains.

Alexander Leslie was waiting for them. He unlocked the gate as William dismounted and walked his mount through the narrow opening to Leslie's inconspicuous lodgings off Market Street. William lifted the prisoner from the horse, cut away his bonds, and then bade him to wait a moment while he led the heated horse a little distance from the vine covered cottage.

A young lad, who was ready and waiting at the stable door, immediately took charge and began rubbing down the pony with cool towels, wiping away the sweat and lather from the harness and bridle. The pony must appear cool and resting.

Tucked away from view and nearly hidden by the wisteria vine, the entrance to the lodging was gated and walled with stone. The narrow close was Leslie's private property. Inaccessible from the Market Street entrance, it was designed with a rear exit leading to a stable with a loft and a hidden cellar.

William and Alexander entered the cottage, and William immediately began divesting himself from the royal guardsman's uniform, while Alexander attended to the needs of the prisoner, so badly in need of food and water.

Dressed in his crofter's disguise, William urged the prisoner to take some food and drink before he whisked him away to the hidden cellar, where they would wait for the outcome of the sudden and dangerous rescue. It could turn ugly if the ruse was discovered, for resistance leaders aiding the Reformation would suffer a death sentence.

The half-starved young man—a vowed priest who had dared to defy and denounce the immorality of the abbey churchmen—was held prisoner in the infamous bottle dungeon. The chilling waters of the North Sea often sprayed over the sea wall, making existence in the stone cell a fate worse than death. Many prisoners held in this notorious dungeon died before ever being brought to trial.

Alleged enemies of the Holy Mother Church must be silenced, suppressed. Any priest who dared to speak out against the immorality in the papal hierarchy was almost, without exception, found guilty of heresy, condemned to death, and quickly executed. The execution site, chosen to accommodate a crowd, was an exhibition of power, meant to strike fear into the hearts of dissenters.

A third conspirator in the rescue attempt, Fergus MacNab, a strapping steel-faced looking Scot with shaggy red hair, led the royal guard from the castle grounds on a lengthy chase from the town. Traveling in a southerly direction onto a narrow road through a dense wood, he rode a Highland Pony not unlike the one used for the rescue. A large bag of barley wheat was thrown across his saddle, secured in place with rough hemp bindings.

When the mounted guards eventually caught up to the supposed rescuer, William Carmichael was riding in the opposite direction of the prisoner. The guard found no more than a simple crofter with a large bag of barley wheat thrown across his saddle.

Enraged and furious, the guards turned their mounts toward the town. They cursed and swore revenge, loudly complaining over their failed attempt to apprehend the prisoner and his liberator, all the while imagining the likely punishment they would receive at the hands of the incensed archbishop.

Laughing with unbridled amusement beneath his red beard and knowing that the real prisoner and Carmichael had supposedly made their escape, Fergus MacNab, his wool cape dotted with beads of rainwater, continued his journey. MacNab rode southward toward the northern edge of the Firth of Forth, where several rivers convened in a large estuary bordered by shoreline villages.

Hidden by his fellow Reformers, the condemned prisoner awaited escape by boat that would whisk him away to England and safety. While King Henry VIII ruled England, a refuge awaited those who had embraced the Protestant Reformation. The outlawed priest would join other Scottish exiles escaping Scotland and certain execution.

From England, some so-called heretics traveled to Geneva or Germany, where they could worship freely without fear of retribution. King Henry VIII offered a refuge to the Protestant Reformers. He hoped to persuade his nephew, King James V of Scotland, to join the Reformation movement, but King James held fast to the Romish religion, while the ravages and repercussions of the Protestant Reformation were ongoing in Scotland.

Chapter 2

*Then I said, I will not make mention of him, nor speak anymore in
his name." But his word was in my heart as a burning fire shut up in
my bones, and I was weary with forbearing, and I could not stay.*

Jeremiah 20:9

AFTER A WEEK OF INTENSE searching along the roads and the
surrounding area for the condemned prisoner and his abductor,
the garrison of Saint Andrews gave up the pursuit. Every croft
and dwelling and every barn and stable in proximity to the town
had been thoroughly searched; but the guard never guessed that
the conspirators were lodged within the town, not far from the
execution site. The ruse had worked, and William and the defrocked
priest escaped during the night, making their way to the fisherman's
boat docked at the harbor.

In 1525, the first law enacted by the Holy Mother Church of Rome
was passed, making the possession of the New Testament in English
and other Protestant literature a crime punishable by death. This
law was passed again in 1535, confirming the death penalty. Heretic
burnings were growing more intense under the heavy hand of the
powerful Archbishop David Beaton. Dissenting priests and Scottish

nobles were watched carefully, and those who spoke out were arrested and tried, like the rescued Benedictine monk.

After seeing the outlawed priest safely on the ship bound for England, William Carmichael left the firth to take ferry boats and the overland journey home to Carmichael. It was a hazardous march, filled with a sense of uneasiness that kept William looking over his shoulder. When he reached the outskirts of West Lothian, he would feel less concerned. The guard would not search that far— or so he thought.

He slept in thickets and shepherd's huts far from the main wagon roads. Meeting the occasional shepherd or farmer on his journey homeward, he accepted their hospitality of food and drink, confident that his crofter's disguise would keep him from being identified as William Carmichael.

The obscure back roads, mere pathways through dense undergrowth, were far safer in planning an escape after rescuing a supposed heretic, preferable for those who knew the forests and glens. The judgments of the Romish Church were harsh and cruel and rarely extended mercy. This rough treatment of the Scottish people by the churchmen of Rome only furthered the spreading division. It ignited the fires of reformation, the insistent cry of the people to be free from corrupt papal rule.

King Henry Vlll of England was a powerful monarch, offering asylum to the convicted Reformation activists. After his divorce from his wife, Catherine of Aragon, and subsequent marriage to Anne Boleyn, he separated himself and England from the ancient domination of papal rule; but he also had personal reasons for refusing to be ruled by the dictates of the Romish Church.

His marriage to Anne Boleyn, a woman in his court who had introduced him to the writings of Luther and the English New Testament, was the king's royal motivation. But before his break from the Holy Mother Church, Henry sought a divorce from the pope of Rome, stating that his marriage to the Spanish princess was cursed because it was not legal. Tragically, all his infant sons by Catherine had died at birth or shortly after, adding credence to this claim.

The pope refused to grant a divorce from his Spanish queen, so King Henry left the ancient religion to declare himself head of the Church of England and sought the divorce from the Archbishop of Canterbury, Thomas Cranmer. After much pressure, the divorce was granted on the grounds that his first marriage to Catherine was not valid. The divorce caused the king to be out of favor with much of Europe; but strangely enough, the English king's break from Rome and his unethical divorce from Catherine served to advance the ongoing Reformation.

In the wake of King Henry's defection from the hierarchy of Rome and his resistance to the counsel of His Holiness, the pope, persecution of the Reformers increased. To rescue condemned Christians for their belief in the biblical truths of the New Testament, teachings that exposed the false traditions long hidden from the people, William Carmichael took up the cause of the Reformation. His mission was to save as many as possible from prison and the stake and to warn the Christian believers if a raid on their secret meetings was imminent.

William remained cautious, meticulous in planning a rescue; but always in the back of his mind was the knowledge that someday, somehow, he might be caught. Someone might betray his trust, accept a bribe, or even be apprehended as a person who might know the real identity of this Reformation Rider, as he had become known. He carefully guarded his identity; and because his home was in proximity to the border regions of Scotland and his well-known family, he was not suspected—at least, not yet.

But for William Carmichael of Carmichael, "Man of the Broken Spear," the risk of this dangerous mission was worth the possibility of capture. At the urging of his brother, Sir John Carmichael, William had curtailed this dangerous work; for he knew that his son, Peter, followed in his footsteps, and the cause of Reformation would not be lost. Even so, a fire burned within his being, glowing with the glorious truth of the gospel, compelling him not to abandon the helpless victims of the archbishop's wrath.

Wasn't it the prophet Jeremiah who vowed never to speak to the people of God again? It seemed all were against the prophet. No one would listen; and he was thrown into prison, persecuted, mocked, and scorned. Even though he vowed to hold back his words and not speak to the people for their lack of obedience, Jeremiah could not stay silent. William remembered those words. They were etched upon his heart; and he carried them on his missions, remembering the prophet: "Then I said, I will not make mention of him, nor speak anymore in his name." But his word was in my heart as a burning fire shut up in my bones, and I was weary with forbearing, and I could not stay."[2]

Like the prophet, William felt the burning in his heart, the ever-present need to warn the believers and to rescue those who were wrongfully imprisoned and sentenced to death at a fiery stake. If only his brother could understand his mission. He had promised Sir John that he would limit his secret activities. But deep inside, the fire burned; and he knew he could not.

---

2   Jeremiah 20:9

Chapter 3

Thou tellest my wanderings: put thou my tears into thy bottle: are they not in thy book? When I cry unto thee, then shall mine enemies turn back: this I know; for God is for me.

Psalm 56:8-9

FEATHERY CLOUDS DRIFTED SLOWLY ACROSS the setting sun, turning the sky pink, gold, and orange and spreading shades of color across the horizon in a brilliant fan of sun-glazed light. From the far side of the lake, Linlithgow Palace was mirrored in the water, reflecting the magnificent sunset until sky and lake seemed as one.

William Carmichael sat astride his mount and watched the fading color of the sunset until the blue and purple of evening shadows fell across the valley. Dismounting his pony, he stretched his weary muscles and rested his back from the aches and pains of the long journey home from Saint Andrews. He was getting older, and he felt it.

From the south side of the lake, he quietly waited, listening and drinking in the breathtaking beauty of evening and the shimmering half-light that illuminated the mist. He remembered how he and Maggie had made it a priority to sit on the terrace of an evening to watch the changing colors of the sunset. But when Maggie had left so suddenly, dying on the day Peter was born, the color in his life had faded, too, just as the sunset faded into misty shadows. Like the hazy gloaming settling over the land, it seemed to settle over his life, too, leaving him with a son to raise and a heart to heal.

The days had turned into years, and Peter had grown to manhood under the guidance of his father and his soldier uncle, Sir John Carmichael of Carmichael. He gathered his thoughts to the present, recalling that he must still navigate the precarious journey homeward.

He stood motionless in the evening mist, listening for any unusual sound, ready to mount his pony. Looking around the immediate area, William caught a glint of something glimmering in the long grass. Out of curiosity, he pushed the grass aside.

A green glass bottle, empty and obviously discarded, lay half-buried in the sticky mud. He picked it up and turned it over, in search of an identifying stamp or etching that was visible; but he found no markings on the smooth glass. Pocketing the small bottle, he swung into the saddle of his pony and turned toward the village of Linlithgow.

In this quaint, little village, he would seek to meet with the family of Henry Forrest, a Benedictine monk martyred for his faith. The family operated a forge and armory and were renowned silversmiths in West Lothian, an area just south of Linlithgow Palace and the picturesque Loch.

The young King James V had been born in this same palace in 1512; and now twenty-six years of age, the youthful and handsome king held tenaciously to the rules and dictates of papal Rome. From the coffers of the abundantly wealthy Roman Church, the king's loyalty to Romish rule was well-rewarded with a yearly stipend and the promise of a marriage negotiation by Catholic France.

The king employed William to oversee the several stables he kept for his blooded horses. In turn, William appointed grooms and trainers to work with every horse and maintained a careful eye on the physical welfare of the royal mounts. Once a month, he inspected the stables and the workers to ensure that adequate care and attention had been maintained in his absence.

William applied this same diligence to the family estate in the southern uplands of Lanarkshire. He kept a careful eye on the borders of Carmichael lands to ensure that cattle reivers—thieves who made their living by stealing, raiding, and pillaging along the border regions of Scotland—did not cross the border into Carmichael lands. His elder brother, Sir John Carmichael, heir to the ancestral estate, depended on William to guard and protect the ancient lands granted to the Carmichaels during the twelfth century, with Glasgow to the northwest and Edinburg to the northeast.

Although not considered Master of the Horse, a position held for years by James Hamilton of Finnart, William was, nevertheless, master of the stable, overseeing every aspect of the king's equestrian obsession. The young King James required his mounts to be prepared and ready for the many festivals, jousts, and royal celebrations so loved by His Majesty.

William would spend some time at the stables with the king's mounts but not before seeking the home of Forrest to beg for a meal and bed for the night. He was tired, exhausted from the stressful rescue of the condemned prisoner at Saint Andrews and the wearisome journey to Linlithgow. He preferred the company of the Forrest family to the rooms at the Linlithgow stables, especially if the king were in residence at the palace.

Thomas Forrest was closing the doors to his smithy for the evening when William walked through the stone enclosure to the open dooryard. William raised a hand in greeting, then led the weary pony over the cobbles and waited.

A slow smile spread across the smithy's jovial face, and he raised his bushy eyebrows in surprise to see William standing in the dooryard. The lines around his eyes and in his forehead were creased with soot, while his blue eyes twinkled from beneath his heavy brows. He was weary from pounding hot iron and was ready to call it a day.

"Aye, so ye have dodged capture once again, eh? And by a gnat's eyelash, no doubt," Thomas said in the way of greeting. "Come, lad, ye look as if ye could use a good meal and a warm bed."

The two men shared the hearty embrace of old friends. "Aye, Thomas, begging your hospitality once again. I could use a good meal, and a bed in the stable will do. I be dog-tired."

"I can see that, lad! The bed in the hayloft is always waiting for ye, hidden away as it is from curious eyes. Be warm as fresh milk, too. But come, William, stable the pony and take some of Iyla's lamb stew before ye sleep. Will put the heart back in ye, lad, indeed it will."

The two men stabled and fed the pony and then entered the cottage where Forrest lived with his wife, Iyla, and their daughter, Lorna. The home, attached to the east side of the smithy and built of thick quarry stone and half-timbered walls, was warmed by the fires of the hot smithy that kept it warm and cozy in winter.

Iyla Forrest was bending over the kitchen fire and lifted a pot of bubbling lamb stew. She set the pot onto the old oak table positioned in the center of the room. When she looked up and saw William, she laughed softly and motioned for him to take a seat next to Thomas.

"Aye, William, so ye be back from your mission with nary a smell of smoke clinging to your cloak!" She carefully wiped her hands on her apron. Tendrils of damp golden-brown hair escaped from beneath her day cap; and she pushed the bothersome strands away from her face, tucking them inside her linen cap.

"Aye, tis so, Iyla, come back unscathed, thanks be to God. And nay, I am not hurt. We were right under the nose of the entire royal regiment; but they could not find us, hidden right in the town—last place they would think to look."

"Good, good, William, and your friends be safe as well?" Iyla queried.

"Hush, woman!" Thomas ordered, glaring at his wife of many years. "The man be half-starved, and there ye be sounding like the bloody inquisition!"

Iyla laughed good-naturedly and handed her formidable husband a wet cloth to wipe his face and hands.

"Ye be on your way to Carmichael then?" Iyla continued.

She winked at William and waved her wooden spoon at her husband, who smiled good-naturedly, despite his wife's persistence.

Slicing a loaf of warm bread, Iyla said sternly, "And hush yourself, husband." She pointed the bread knife at Thomas.

Thomas and William laughed at Iyla's idle threat, and Iyla joined in the good-natured banter. The fragrant odor of crusty bread and the pot of warm stew caused William's mouth to water. He was so tired and so in need of this pleasant and hospitable table.

"Someday, lad," Iyla continued, "I fear ye shall not be so blessed as to escape the old reprobate cardinal's grasp; but praise be to God, ye are safe thus far."

"Aye, that be so, Iyla, that be so. I promised Sir John if I returned successful this time, I would cut back on me missions." He smiled. "I be getting too old, not as quick as I once was. Peter will have to carry on."

Thomas took a slice of the warm bread and began sopping up his stew. "If the lad be as zealous as his da', he can carry on, that be certain."

"Nay, Thomas," said Iyla reproachfully. "Let God be thanked before ye take another bite like some heathen." She nodded in William's direction. "If ye be so kind, William, please bless our humble fare."

"Aye, Iyla," William agreed.

The three friends bowed their heads; and William began to pray in a somewhat wearisome tone, his hands trembling slightly from hunger and fatigue.

"Our heavenly Father, we indeed be thankful for this meal prepared by our friend, Iyla. Bless her, Thomas, and Lorna—this home—and keep it safe from any who would try to spoil it. Ye know, Lord, that loyalty binds us together like thorns to the thistle. Give us faith and grant us mercy, for who of us can 'hold the wind in his fists' or gather up the waters in his cloak?3 Nay, we can do nothing unless ye be with us. Hold us close, for we be your children. Amen."

During the prayer, the door opened quietly, and Lorna Forrest slipped inside the warm cottage and waited in silence until William finished the mealtime blessing.

William stood in respect to a lady; but Lorna waved a hand and motioned for him to stay seated, then took her accustomed place at the table while smiling a greeting to her parents.

Genuine relief lifted Lorna's lips into a warm smile at seeing her friend return unharmed from his dangerous mission. "I am happy to

---

3   Proverbs 30:4

see ye, William, sitting at our table with Mama and Da'. God has been good—as always."

"Thank ye lass, and aye, thanks be to God. It was a difficult mission, but God was with us. By now, the condemned priest has safely escaped to England or the continent."

The kettle steamed, and a fragrant odor filled the room. Iyla sliced thick wedges of fresh baked bread and thin slices of golden cheese and then said, "There's plenty now, so eat hearty. Lorna worked at the armory today, testing out some new weapons—her favorite thing to do, ye kin. That's why she be late to supper."

"A blessing for me that she fired her weapon with amazing accuracy at that ugly royal guardsman aiming to kill me," William offered. "Ye kin, after we fled from that bloody trial. That be several years ago now, but it seems like yesterday. I would be a dead man if Lorna had not been there."

A sense of great sadness fell over the friends gathered at the table at the mention of the day Henry Forrest, a son and brother of this well-loved family, was martyred, burned at the stake for speaking out against the corrupt practices of the Romish hierarchy. Memories of the grief and hurt were never far from their minds. Forrest was condemned to death by the wicked ruling of Archbishop Beaton. He was burned as a traitor and a heretic, but his dying words of faith in the gospel was a constant comfort to the grieving family.

Thomas Forrest had sent his daughter on this dangerous journey to beg the Archbishop Beaton for mercy for his son. But Lorna was pushed aside by the royal guard who warned her to stop interfering with the execution proceedings, or she would be arrested. She had fled to a hill overlooking the execution site and hid herself in the dense undergrowth to await the outcome of her brother's trial.

Being enlightened to the truths of the gospel discovered in Tyndale's English New Testament, Forrest had been brought before the council and judged a heretic. A daring attempt by William Carmichael to rescue the young Benedictine monk had failed. Forrest was condemned for his declaration of faith; and despite William's valiant efforts to save him, the young man had died in the flames of martyrdom.

After the rescue had failed, William rode his pony away, escaping capture by the royal guard searching for the would-be rescuer. When he neared Lorna's hiding place, he had discovered the lass hiding in the brush. Realizing she was Forrest's sister, William had encouraged the grieving lass to leave the area quickly before they both were discovered. They had made ready to travel south to West Lothian, where they would be safe.

Before the couple could get away, the royal guard came upon them; and an altercation of swords followed. William easily dispatched the first guard, but the second guard was stronger and quite determined. Although a furious exchange of blows followed, the guard had managed to sink his sword into William's thigh as he fought to protect Lorna.

William had bled profusely and lost strength from the deep gash in his leg. Then suddenly and with deadly accuracy, a pistol shot had run out from the trees where Lorna was hiding. With one well-aimed shot to the head, Lorna had shot the guard, killing him instantly. She had saved Williams' life.

Lorna broke the sudden silence at the supper table by diverting the talk away from her brother's execution. "Nay, Mama I'm just in time. Finished the last testing and all is working well. William can tell us about his . . . ah . . . adventure. It is his to tell if he wishes to share it."

Lifting her eyes to William, Lorna noted the weariness written on his features. She remembered to be careful about knowing or speaking of his dangerous mission to save as many believers as possible from the cardinal's wrath.

William sighed. "I be sorry, me friends, for calling to mind the hurt of that bloody day. I hoped and prayed the outcome had been different, that I could have . . . could have . . . "

He left off speaking; and taking a deep breath, he looked around at his friends, their eyes reflecting sympathy for his feelings of regret. They understood what words could not convey.

"Sometimes," William continued, "I become so exhausted with the effort of it all, I speak carelessly, ye kin. Forgive me."

"Och, lad, there is nothing to forgive," Thomas said. "We understand. Ye did your best. That is what matters, ye kin. Perilous times these, perilous times.

"Aye," Thomas said, pausing momentarily to study William's rugged features, "we mourn the loss of our Henry, of all believers who left the old religion to believe the truth of the gospel of Jesus Christ, the true gospel. Och," he said, exhaling a long, ragged breath, "and more's the pity, died for it, too."

"Well, lad, ye be weary from your long journey—and rightly so. Dinna fash yourself overmuch," Iyla offered encouragingly. "We— none of us—fault ye."

They finished the meal and talked of Lorna's day at the armory, where she was testing the newly forged Highland pistol. She was an expert shot and could shoot an arrow accurately with a bow that she had fashioned herself. They talked of the king's marriage to Marie de Guise of France and how the marriage would affect the young king. Within Scotland, political and spiritual tensions were rapidly escalating in the governing powers that dictated the future of Scotland.

Chapter 4

Jesus said unto him, If thou canst believe,
all things are possible to him that believeth.

Mark 9:23

SUPPER ENDED, AND IYLA AND Lorna cleared the table and then gathered some clean linen to make up the small spare room for William; but he refused to stay in the cottage, preferring instead a bed in the hayloft of the stable, a warm and cozy place hidden away, unobserved by any who might happen by. William was a cautious man, always sleeping with his dirk and sword at the ready.

Together, William and Lorna stepped through the low door of the half-timbered croft and carefully scanned the premises to make certain none of the king's men were about. Then, they entered the stables, Lorna holding the bedding in her arms and William carrying a bucket of warm water with soap and towels. He was grimy, battered from the rigors of the trail; and a bath would feel wonderful after the long trek from Saint Andrews.

With the bucket of warm water in one hand, William climbed the narrow wooden ladder to the hayloft pungent with the odors of sweet-smelling fodder. His presence unsettled the birds sleeping in the rafters and set them to peeping. Knowing the intruder meant no harm, they tucked their heads under their wings again and settled down to sleep.

William smiled, thinking how he preferred the companionship of birds to those he met on the homeward trail. Like the wee birds, that's what he intended to do—tuck his head under the blankets and settle down to sleep. He was in a safe place, far from the dangers of the trail. He would soon be back safely at Carmichael.

William descended the ladder, returning to the lower level to gather up the woolen bedding. He hoped for a quiet rest, unobserved by somebody looking over his shoulder. He smiled as he watched Lorna grooming her pony. She met his gaze and smiled back, her eyes glowing.

Lorna lovingly stroked the long nose of her own chocolate-colored mare, Velvet, as she slipped the beast a dried apple from last year's winter store. She laughed softly as the mare pushed her nose under her shawl in search of more treats.

William's admiration of Lorna was evident. After all, she possessed amazing strength and courage in traveling alone to Saint Andrews to watch the execution of her only brother, hoping against hope that somehow, he would be spared.

He vividly recalled how accurately she had sent a bullet straight into the forehead of the royal guardsman ready to dispatch him, thereby saving his life at the last moment, a feat she didn't care to remember. He smiled as he remembered how he had thought Lorna was a man hiding in the bushes. When he had pulled her from the tangle of brush, he had discovered a lass, trembling with fright, alone, and weeping with grief.

A Highland pistol was tucked in her belt, the very same pistol she fired in time to save his life. He never quite understood why she hadn't shot him when he reached for her and pulled her from her hiding place. Perhaps she had sensed that he was not an enemy but someone who could help her.

"Enos groomed your pony," Lorna said. Turning to William while stroking the mare, she continued, "So you can rest safely enough tonight before working with the king's mounts tomorrow. His men from Linlithgow stables are often here at the forge, bringing their mounts for Da' to fit shoes and repair harnesses, even though they have their own smithy. Da' is the best."

William looked thoughtful and paused to study his surroundings, his hazel eyes exploring the shaded corners of the stable as though he expected someone might be hidden there. Peering at William from beneath her dark lashes, Lorna noted his cautious and vigilant manner.

"All is well, William, I assure you," said Lorna. "The stables have been searched, and there is nothing here to cause you concern. Our stable man, Enos, inspects the stables and the premises nightly."

Sighing, William said, "Aye, lass, I be so long on this journey . . . find it hard to trust anyone. I truly be sorry." His brow wrinkled into a frown. "So close to home yet I have no peace until I be in me own bed, and even then . . . " Finding it hard to express his thoughts, he broke off speaking.

"I do understand, my friend," she said wistfully. "I feel the same, even in my own bed. After Henry was martyred, I was discovered watching those unlawful proceedings by Cardinal Beaton's royal guard. And then, after the murder of that guard and our escape, I have not been at peace, William. Nay, I fear retribution."

She paused, laying the grooming brushes onto a shelf. Then, looking sadly at William, she continued, "I fear they will come for me someday—the magistrates—even though I do not think they connected me with Henry. But then, maybe they did. The guard here are not the same men who are at Saint Andrews."

"What ye did was not murder, Lorna," he said sternly. "It was self-defense, self-preservation. Ye should not accept blame for what ye could not prevent, ye kin. Aye, it is always hard to take a life, even if the man is a despicable rogue. Dinna fash yourself, lass." At his words, her eyes brimmed with unshed tears.

Hoping to ease her fears, William said tenderly, "Difficult times, they cause us to do things—things not in our heart to do, choices we must make—that in another situation, we would readily refuse."

"In some respects, ye are right; but, William, my mind goes back to Lady Janet Douglas, and she was innocent. All knew that. Still, she was executed merely because she was a Douglas, not because she conspired to poison the king. I remember—"

"Do not go there, Lorna," he said, interrupting her thought. "'Tis a waste of time to compare yourself with the Countess of Glamis, Lady Janet. After all, she was sister-in-law to the Earl of Angus, the king's hated enemy, reason enough in his own wicked mind to burn her as a witch. Truth be told, he wanted her estates for his own ungodly greed."

He sighed, shaking his head in disbelief, then continued, "After Sir John rescued Katherine from the king's court, James grew more perverse and signed the death warrant for Lady Janet. I believe guilt drives him to unstable acts of hostility and depression. The Court fears him, says he has bouts of paranoia, talks to himself, seeking forgiveness for unnamed terrors that plague him in the night hours.

Clearly, the king's behavior does not deserve your consideration, not at all."

"Aye, but it does. Since Lady Janet was executed, the king's men have been questioning women who make natural remedies for healing, even suggesting that anyone involved in what they call alchemy—using herbs for healing—could be a witch. I have made herbal remedies for years, William, but now I fear to have them available for my neighbors and friends. It is too risky, too frightening."

Tears flooded her eyes, and she turned away, not wanting William to see her distress. "And then," she said turning back to look at William, "since Da' has denounced the superstition of the Romish Church, losing faith in all he had previously believed, we will surely be a target for heresy by Rome's degree."

"Nay, lass. Your father is far too valuable. His skills as a silversmith and blacksmith for the king will protect him from his enemies. And there is the armory, an asset worthy of the king's protection. Fear not, Lorna. God is watching over your family."

Lorna ran her hand along the smooth side of the mare's face and patted it gently in a farewell gesture. "I trust God will not fail us, William." She sighed. "It has been so difficult to keep faith after Henry was burnt, but I found comfort in God's Word today."

"Aye, lass, His word is always a blessing to we pilgrims, granting us a respite for our journey through life. It is our refuge, our safe place, our encouragement through these perilous times."

She brushed her hands on the folds of her skirt. "I read in Isaiah this morning—the old Vulgate version in Latin approved by the pope—'they that wait upon the Lord shall renew their strength; they shall mount up with wings as eagles; they shall run, and not be weary; and they shall walk, and not faint.[4] I felt the Lord was trying to help me have faith in Him when I feel helpless and weak."

"We do have a Comforter, lass. I am weary myself, and it is well that ye shared your trouble with me. I needed to hear that Scripture, too. And, Lorna, ye are not weak as ye imagine. Ye are a strong woman, a brave woman, ye kin, blessed by God."

At his kind words, she smiled, her eyes shining with affection. "And now, William, I must go. I have taken too much of your time when you need to rest. Tomorrow, you will inspect the king's stables, and then you must go home to Carmichael, to your family. Peter will be eager to see his da' again, to make certain you are safe."

"Aye, they be anxious when I am away," William said and paused, for he knew his job was extremely dangerous, reason enough for them to worry. "Ye never know what might happen. In a month or so, I will return to Linlithgow to inspect the king's stables."

"In another month, ye say?" Lorna sounded uneasy, like she feared trouble.

"Try not to fret, lass. God is helping the believers, and, Lorna, ye are special—special to God." Then, softly, he said, "And special to me." Placing one hand against her soft cheek in farewell and not daring to speak what he felt stirring in his heart, he dropped his hand and said, "Goodnight, lass, and God be with ye."

"And with you," Lorna whispered, her dark brown eyes shining as if they held some mystery in their depths. Then, she quietly walked to the side entrance of the stable, well-hidden from any passersby. Opening the door, she turned to face him and said, "Your bath water

---

4   Isaiah 40:31

will be cold, William, and don't forget to pull the ladder up into the loft for the night." Without another word, she exited the stable, slipping quietly into the misty evening of another Scottish springtime.

Chapter 5

Be ready always to give an answer to every man that asketh you a reason of the hope that is in you with meekness and fear.

1 Peter 3:15

SIR JOHN CARMICHAEL PACED THE oak floor of his private study—the war room, he called it—a room filled with the trappings of battles won and lost, remembrances of warfare and brutal conflict. Shields and swords hung on the paneled walls, and a broken spear was mounted on the chimney breast above the oak mantel of the huge inglenook stone fireplace. To the casual observer, the broken spear was an unusual memorial of some ancient battle.

Beneath the damaged spear, the Carmichael Clan crest, embellished with the same symbol of a broken spear, was central. Despite its broken state, the spear was prominently displayed with the crest in the center.

Sir John stopped his pacing for a moment, his eyes coming to rest on the fractured spear over the mantel. Pausing, he glanced around at the four walls with steely blue eyes as though he were contemplating the significance of the vast displays of weaponry. William was late returning to Carmichael, and he was worried and wondering if he had managed to escape capture.

His wolfhound, Zebulon, his head resting lightly on his paws, waited patiently by the fireside hearth. His wary eyes followed Sir John's moves. The dog sensed his master's unease; but no command had been given, and he was an obedient and faithful companion to Sir John.

A private man, Sir John was considered by many to be somewhat austere, discreet, and serious in his demeanor, shrewd and careful in managing the Carmichael estate in the southern uplands of Scotland. He was the heir of a long dynasty of Carmichaels, the eldest of his family, a soldier born and bred for battle.

His rugged features—strong, robust, and solid—seemed to be carved in granite and reflected a presence of power and authority. He was tall and powerfully built with a purely masculine appearance. A black and silver beard covered his rugged features, and a leather band held his salt-and-pepper hair at the nape of his neck. Intense blue eyes were set beneath hooded brows that dominated his broad forehead. But his eyes were kind, and his curved lips smiled easily. When he spoke, his voice was deep and gravelly.

Outside the tall window facing north, raindrops beat against the glass panes and slowly slid down the glass in long rivulets of water. Amid the mist and the raindrops, a figure on horseback rode to the back terrace, where a side door at the end of the hallway exited the keep to the kitchen garden. It was William. A stable lad ran through the pelting rain to grab his horse; and then William proceeded to the side door, not wanting their housekeeper, Coira, to see his wet and tattered condition. She would scold him like a mother and call for a hot bath and warm soup.

Opening the heavy oak door to his study, Sir John stepped into the hallway, where William was entering the keep through the side door. He glanced at his brother and shook his head slightly, his eyebrows raised; but his face registered relief.

"Och, brother," Sir John said in way of greeting, "if the magistrates don't get you, this abominable weather will. Get out of those wet clothes, and I'll stir up the fire."

Laughing, William agreed. "Aye, John, it was a deluge, a constant downpour for the last five miles." He shook himself like a wet dog and then reached down to pat Zebulon, who was greeting him with a series of short barks. The dog was fairly dancing, his dog-like joy evident.

"Nay, Zebulon, hush, ye will blow me cover, and Coira will be here in a thrice to scold us both. Ye know how it is, John," William said. "Best I clean up a wee bit before she discovers me. When I get out of these wet clothes, be back with the news."

"Aye, William. First thing, get yourself dry." Sir John returned to the study and stirred up the hot embers in the fireplace. He added more wood; and soon, a crackling fire sprang to life, sending sparks hurling upward. His brother had returned, and he felt great relief knowing that William was home safe once again.

A soft knock at the door and Coira, the housekeeper and all-around household organizer of all things, opened the door and came in carrying a large tray filled with a bowl of steaming stew, hot biscuits, and a kettle of hot cider. She placed it on the table near the window and turned to Sir John.

"Aye, Sir John, I saw the lad come riding in like a man possessed and sneak in the back hall. Mind ye, I expected no less, even after all me warnings. He persists in riding out in all manner of weather."

"He did not want to trouble ye, Coira. He was soaked, all wet and muddy, dripping all over the flagstones," said Sir John with a crooked smile.

"So headstrong he is—just like your da', only a mite sweeter." She threw up her hands in exasperation and turned to leave; but in an instant, she turned again. "Be sure, Sir John, he eats the hot food. There be hot tea and cider. Will scare off the chills. Heaven knows there has been enough dyin' in this family, and I dinna think I can bare another."

"I will see to it, Coira, and thank ye for your kind concern. I be sorry that William seems, well, a wee bit contrary to your motherly warnings. He appears careless; but he does what he does, and not even I can change him."

"Aye, I be knowin' that, Sir John. But I was at the bedside of your sweet mama when she drew her last breath, and I promised her," Coira added with a tremor in her voice, "to care for ye and William. And I do me best to keep ye both alive. Truth be told, I love ye both, like me own sons; and me being only a few years older than ye—a great hulking bairn to care for—but I promised, and well ye know it."

His eyes softening, Sir John said, "Dinna fash yourself overmuch, Coira. Remember, I was a grown man when Mama died, and William, a young willful lad. Ye have done well to keep our household running smoothly and efficiently, aye, and we love ye for it. Now, send a housemaid to clean up the hall and do not fret so. The tray of hot food is much appreciated."

Tears glistened in the aging housekeeper's eyes as she bobbed a wee curtsey and left the study.

Sir John recounted her tearful words. *Heaven knows there has been enough dyin' in this family.* And Coira had been there to witness it all. She had come as a young woman from Ireland to manage the household at Carmichael House and soon became the hub of the home, caring and nurturing, overseeing every detail of running the home, and taking on a motherly role when her mistress had died too young.

Now, both parents were gone, a generation passed, resting beneath the trees on Kirk Hill. Then, unbelievably, his own sweet Gwendolyn had died and then William's wife, Maggie, both women dying from complications of childbirth and leaving behind two infants to care for.

Those were dark days for Clan Carmichael, and it was Coira who had taken on the role of mother to William's son, Peter, and Katherine, Sir John's own sweet daughter. They were cousins but raised like brother and sister. Coira was right—there had been enough dying in their family.

Like many men who lost their wives to the difficulties of childbirth, not to mention the ravages of disease and plague, death was always lurking in the shadows. Neither Sir John nor William had looked for a wife to wed again. In his earlier years, Sir John was often away soldiering in some part of Scotland or even on the continent, so his wee Katherine and William's son, Peter, had grown up under Coira's guiding hand. But Coira, now in her seventies, was turning many of her household responsibilities over to younger housemaids, training them to someday take over her duties.

William returned to the study after donning dry clothes and tying back his hair neatly. Choosing a chair next to the hearth, he rubbed his hands together and enjoyed the warmth of the fire blazing on the grate. He breathed in the fragrant odors of hot food, and his mouth watered.

Leaving the warmth of the fireside, he filled a wooden trencher with savory hot stew and biscuits and then poured himself a large mug of fragrant cider. He sat down at the small table near the window to enjoy the warm food and steaming spicy cider.

"Well, looks like Coira caught me riding in, no doubt, then hurried to fetch some warm food and drink before I be catching a chill," William remarked while dipping a biscuit in the savory stew. He smiled at Sir John. Raising his eyebrows, Sir John chuckled.

William was tall with hard sinewy muscles, leaner in build than his soldier brother. He resembled Sir John; but his features were sharper, more chiseled, and his face was smoothly shaven. He was a ruggedly handsome man with striking hazel eyes set in aristocratically carved features. He wore his dark, wavy hair tied back for donning the many wigs he used to disguise himself as a simple crofter or farmer. Thus disguised, he rode about the country warning the secret believers of an impending raid on their meeting sites.

Sir John helped himself to a mug of spiced cider and sat down opposite William. "Aye, Coira saw you riding up and began to fret over your cold, wet condition. Och, ye know she worries over us. But here ye are at last with a warm fire and hot food. Now tell me of your rescue and obvious escape."

Nodding between bites, William said, "Well, the rescue went off without a hitch. We kept the poor, beaten wretch—a priest who spoke out against the immorality of the clergy—at Leslie's hidden close, right under the nose of the inquisitors. The man was in bad shape, John, half-starved and savagely beaten." William sighed and shook his head.

"Had to wait some days for him to recover, ye kin. He was in no shape to travel." Pushing his trencher aside, William paused to stare out the window.

Sir John sipped his cider, his face an indiscernible mask; but his steely blue eyes sparked fire at the brutality leveled at the so-called rebellious priest. He absently patted Zebulon's head as he waited for William to resume the tale. Zebulon cocked his head, turning it back and forth as though listening to William's account.

"After snatching up the priest," William continued, "I rode me pony away with the priest across me saddle and made off before the guard and the churchmen knew what was happening. Fergus MacNabb, one of our men, waited for the signal that all was well and then led the royal garrison on a wild goose chase west of Saint Andrews.

"I can tell ye, brother, Beaton and his churchmen were spittin' mad. Several days later, MacNabb returned to Leslie's close by night to spirit the priest away. Then, he then took him to the coast to board a ship bound for England. The believers planned it all from there. God was with us."

William sighed heavily. He was exhausted with recounting the details of the amazing rescue of the condemned priest. His bones ached, and his muscles tightened with the strain of riding for miles in the inclement weather. A great lump rose in his throat, and his hazel eyes shimmered with unshed tears. The journey, the rescue, and the possibility of capture left him emotionally spent.

"Thankfully, John, I be safe home, ever so grateful to be done with such a risky scheme and eager to get away. Took the less traveled trails to safety and rode miles through the rain just to be with me own family again." He shuddered involuntarily. The danger of the daring raid and his own escape were still too real.

"Aye, me brother, and I pray this will be your last mission for a while. Perhaps, it is time for ye to let the Reformation Rider retire from these dangerous missions. There are other ways to serve, William."

A slight frown creased Sir John's brow. After all, his brother was not a young man anymore. William's passion for the Reformation in Scotland was still a burning fire, a fire that could easily burn out of control. Although his identity was well-hidden, undiscovered by even the locals, and was known only to a few trusted men, if he were ever caught, he would forfeit his life. The magistrates had been looking for the Reformation Rider for years, and their frustration at being unable to find him was evident.

"Of course, rescuing the prisoner priest from the hands of that wicked archbishop was thankworthy," offered Sir John, "but I fear Peter is following the same dangerous mission. He is forming a network of resistance believers, men he trusts, to further the cause of the Reformation and, perhaps, overtake the religious stronghold at Saint Andrews."

"Overtake Saint Andrews?"

"Aye, that be the rumor."

"Och, I be hearing such blather. But the area is well-fortified; and unless one could take the castle itself, there would be no way to break through such a strong defense. This idea is just wishful thinking on the part of the overzealous Resistance believers."

"And haven't I told ye all along that taking up arms to fight this religious war is not wise, nor do I feel it is God's way?"

"Aye, John, ye have told me countless times."

Sir John pushed his chair back and stood. He began to pace, then stopped in mid-stride and turned to face William, who was pushing the empty bowl of stew away, waiting for his older brother to begin the lecture. "Brother, for years, we have managed to avoid being accused of heresy—as the pope names it—even though the entire of Carmichael has been searched several times. But, William, how long will we remain so? Think of the consequences."

"I do think of them, John, but I feel impressed by God to help in this great cause to spare the believers and to stop the papal tyranny."

"I be grieved to belabor the point, William, but I see no clear path through this treacherous spiritual warfare. All we can do is pray, leave it with God, and trust Him to fight this battle."

"And we be back to the same difference of opinion on the matter, John. Ye kin, let us not speak of this anymore. Please, John. I am exhausted. We can talk of this later."

"Nay, William. Let us finish, and you can rest."

Chapter 6

Trust in the Lord with all thine heart; and lean not unto thine own understanding. In all they ways, acknowledge Him and He shall direct thy paths.

Proverbs 3:5-6

SIGHING DEEPLY, WILLIAM ROSE TO his feet, his facial features lined with weariness. "John, I know we have different views on how to proceed—and aye, I understand what ye are saying—but we canna give up the fight for freedom from tyranny and injustice. There must be a way; and if it comes to arms, then let it come."

"Let it come to arms, William? Are ye daft?"

"Me heart is in this, John. Didn't God tell Joshua to be strong and courageous, not to fear or be discouraged? Won't God be with us as He was with Joshua? Remember, John, Joshua was going into a literal battle."

"Aye, William, in Joshua's time, that was true; but Jesus speaks of peace, of conquering our enemies with the Sword of the Spirit. We must believe ourselves to be in God's hands; and live or die, we are the Lord's. There are too many admonishments in the Word of God that warn us to be at peace with all men. Job says, 'At destruction and famine thou shalt laugh: neither shall thou be afraid of the beasts of the earth.'"[5]

"Well, I may be laughing, and I've had enough of beasts who put in prison and burn believers for simply reading the English New Testament."

Frustration only added to William's reason. Wanting to end this conversation, he ran his finger through his hair and added, "But I promise ye this, John. I will pray for another way, someone God will raise out of this darkness to continue me work, a necessary work as I see it."

Sir John's eyes softened with compassion. He spoke of his worst fear. "And what if that man were Peter? What then, William? I told ye that Peter was gathering a network of believers for this very cause. Would ye wish him to be part of a physical war that might cost him his life?"

"Nay, of course not, but I canna say whom God will call, John. Peter is ready; he is strong and careful and has a heart that is true. I canna prevent what God will ordain." He shook his head slowly, realizing that the future was unclear, the path ahead uncertain.

"At this moment, me brother, I be too weary to sort it out. Be patient with me, and we will talk it out another day. I be too exhausted for more talk, and I canna think clearly."

The subject ended just as it always had—two brothers with different opinions but both brothers deeply devout, searching for wisdom, and hoping for deliverance from the religious tyranny now ruling Scotland.

"Vera well, William. Ye must rest, ye kin."

---

5   Job 5:22

"And by the way, John, where is Peter, wee John, and Katherine? Are they not still here at Carmichael?"

"Peter traveled south to the middle marches to speak on our behalf with the Wardens of the Scottish Marches. "Spring is here, and the reivers are active again. The Wardens of the March, both Scottish and English, are planning a Truce Day for the clans on both sides of the border."

"Ha! Such a fruitless effort for a Truce Day," William said. "It is a mockery and never works. Soon as the truce is declared and the Wardens leave, border clans start fighting and raiding again."

Sir John shrugged his shoulders and nodded his head in agreement. "Aye, it be always the same. And Katherine is at Cowthally Castle with wee John. Lady Somerville is preparing for the Rid Hose Race, and Katherine is helping with the details of planning the footrace. She will be going into confinement soon after the race, ye remember."

"Aye, I remember," said William. "God bless our dear Katherine and give her a safe delivery."

"Robbie is participating," continued Sir John, "and Peter will join us there when he returns from Truce Day. We must go to the event, of course." Sir John laughed, his base voice echoing. "It is always a jolly time."

"The Somervilles will soon be celebrating the birth of their first grandchild," said William smiling.

"Aye, and Robbie is eager that all goes well with the birthing, truth be told. Lady Somerville will be there and several midwifes—or so I'm told."

Sir John smiled sadly and dismissed the earlier conversation with William to wait for another day. God must guide them through the dark days ahead, and they were both committed to the cause of reformation, although by different means. They faced each other, paused, and listened to the rain beating a rhythm against the window as they allowed the silence to absorb their fears.

Then, the brothers embraced fondly, remembering their pledge, a vow never to allow anything or anyone to separate them. After all, they were "Men of the Broken Spear," bound by honor and, if possible, always ready to right the wrong.

William stretched, yawned, and then left the study to get some much-needed rest.

Chapter 7

Tell the ladies only of brave knights and heroic courage.

COWTHALLY CASTLE, HOME OF THE Somervilles, was in the parish of Carnwath, the name meaning "cairn in the woods." Over the years, the castle was enlarged and remodeled; and a deep, double moat with a wide drawbridge was added to protect the three towers of the keep. Thick stone walls surrounded the keep with the only entrance to the castle on the west side. Inside the outer wall, an exterior courtyard housed a blacksmith's shop, cartwright sheds, animal shelters, and the stables. An extensive garden near the keep enhanced the beauty of Cowthally Castle with aromatic herbs and a variety of colorful flowers.

Until his untimely death at the Battle of Flodden in 1513, King James IV was a frequent visitor to Cowthally Castle, where he enjoyed the hospitality of the Somervilles and hunting with his falcons on the extensive estates. He was a popular ruler, energetic and vigorous in his devotion to Scotland. He united the Scottish clans under his royal control, strengthened the struggling finances, and was a presence in the political realm.

His heir, James V, crowned king as an infant at the time of his father's death, Scotland was ruled by Scottish lords and regents until the time he would reach his majority. His mother's second husband, the sixth Earl of Angus, Archibald Douglas, took advantage of the child king and held him captive for two years. While James was in captivity, the Earl of Angus showered him with gifts and introduced him to inappropriate and disreputable pleasures.

James despised his former stepfather; and when he was just sixteen, he escaped from Angus and began to rule Scotland as its rightful heir. When he began his reign, he continued his father's love of hunting and was often at the vast estate owned by the Somervilles.

In 1524, Sir Hugh, the fifth Lord of Cowthally Castle, built a great hall to entertain his royal guests. Among those who came to Carnwath to hunt was the young James V, now king of Scots. While the young king was hunting with his falcons, he was often in the company of Katherine Carmichael, Sir John's only daughter. James had fallen in love with the young and vivacious Katherine; but he could never marry her, for she was not of royal blood. Nevertheless, he pursued her with passion.

After her mother's untimely death, Katherine was under the protection of Lady Somerville, a virtuous woman who guarded Katherine's virtue from the young king's advances. When Katherine refused the king's continual pursuit of her favor, the frustrated King James V issued a royal summons requiring Katherine to come to court as his mistress.

The summons could not be refused, despite Sir John Carmichael's objections. Her only option was to flee into exile. Katherine had refused exile and lived at the royal court for five years. The couple had one son, John Stewart, one of the king's many illegitimate children; but nevertheless, wee Johnny was loved and cherished by the Carmichaels and Somervilles.

And now, years after Katherine had been released from the king's court and had married her first love, Robbie Somerville, she sat before the fire of the private solar located above the great hall. Lady Somerville and Katherine had volunteered to sew the flags for the Red Hose Race. They chatted amicably, their needles flying as they worked.

"I just love how you have made the great hall look so elegant, so fresh and springy," Katherine said to Lady Somerville. "Those beautiful tapestries and paintings of the deer and falcon hunt are just stunning.

"Aye," agreed Lady Somerville, "we added the new tapestries and paintings of the Scottish countryside to offset our grim looking ancestors." She laughed and pointed to a recently relocated painting of an especially sour-looking man holding a sober-faced child.

"Why the artists paint these portraits with eyes following you everywhere is a mystery to me. Perhaps it is to scare the mice away," she said laughing. "You know, Katherine, Sir Hugh likes to show off his great hall, ye kin."

"Aye, tis so," Katherine said taking in the gloomy looking portrait. "Well, Sir Hugh has a right to be proud. He is such a congenial host, so generous and thoughtful of his guests. I am expecting him to provide an equally bountiful feast at the end of the race. Who will be in attendance, dear lady?"

"Well, Katherine," Lady Somerville said pausing in her sewing and laying her needles in her lap. "I hope this doesn't distress you. But King James and his wife all but invited themselves, and of course, Sir Hugh couldn't refuse them."

"Oh," Katherine said, her face reddening with the news. "Of course, Sir Hugh couldn't refuse the king. It is just rather . . . well, rather awkward whenever we happen to meet. And his wife, Marie, is wary of me—naturally so. But he does like to see wee Johnny. After all, he is the king's own son—although, not a legitimate heir—but he does seem to love him just the same."

"Of course, he loves him. I daresay that he seems to love all his children, despite their ignoble beginnings. I understand he has seven children now, all by his mistresses." She sighed, regretting the mention of this kingly prerogative to keep mistresses, despite warnings from the pope and those who considered this practice immoral and corrupt.

"And, Katherine," Lady Somerville added, "do not worry. No one can resist your sweet boy, and Robbie adores him. Now that the king is married to Marie de Guise, he is hoping for a legitimate heir—a son, of course—to inherit the throne of Scotland."

How easily his other children were relegated to insignificance when an heir was born thought Katherine. She remembered the years she was at court, the unwilling mistress to the king. He had showered her with gifts, was kind and caring; but when wee Johnny was born, he had looked at him as just another offspring of his carnal pleasure.

"But if it is any comfort, other lairds and gentry will attend as well, Katherine—nearly a hundred guests—so there will be enough entertainment for our king and his lady to stay occupied."

"Will they stay on after the race?" Katherine queried.

"From what I understand, they will not attend the race but are coming for the hunting and hawking a few days later," said Lady Somerville with a measure of hope. She picked up her needles and began to stitch. "You can always return to Carmichael House after the race and the feast following if you feel too uncomfortable."

"Nay, dear Lady," Katherine said softly, "I will not return to Carmichael this close to my confinement, so do not worry over me. We planned to have the babe here at Cowthally; and Lord willing, it will be as we have planned."

"That seems right, Katherine, and hopefully, the babe will not make an appearance until all our guest have returned to their homes."

Katherine sighed, a wistful look crossing her features. "When Papa requested that I return to Carmichael after the king chose a wife, I tried to forget . . . forget I was Jamie's reluctant mistress. And if it were not for wee Johnny, I may have been able to ignore that part of my life." Tears brimmed in her eyes, and she turned her face away and looked through the tall window, where new velvet hangings were swept to one side allowing the sun to shine through the stained glass.

"Och, sweet lass," Lady Somerville said soothingly. "You have shed enough tears over that relationship, and you must put it to rest—not only for your good but for Robbie's peace of mind as well."

"Aye, I understand this, dear lady. But even if I could put it from my mind, we have a child together; so in some respects, we shall always be connected, like it or not."

"I understand, Katherine. But you are married to Robbie now; and he loves you so much, just as he always has. And now, you are expecting this new babe, a blessing from God. Take joy in this, Katherine. The Word of God says to forget 'those things which are behind, and reaching forth unto those things which are before.'"[6]

"I am trying every day," Katherine said with a sigh. "But when I see the king on occasion—when he visits wee Johnny—those days at court come flooding back. I tried to influence him to have mercy

---

6   Philippians 3:13

and spare the believers. It was my entire purpose to acquiesce to that royal summons; but in the end, it was a futile effort—or so it seems."

With a slight smile, Katherine turned to her mother-in-law, her voice soft and her eyes still brimming. "However, dear lady, I do appreciate your counsel and will do my best to be a good wife to Robbie. He has been such a support, and I do love him, always have."

"Well, I promised your dear mother when you were born to do my best to guide your future, to give you counsel when needed. And now, not only am I your mother-in-law but also soon to be grandmother to this new babe, our first grandson. We are all so thankful, so blessed."

Katherine brushed her tears away and laughed. "You are certain this babe is a boy? And if it is a lass, will you still be happy?"

Lady Somerville smiled broadly. "Och, lass, well of course, of course! A lass will be just as welcome. I just seem to think it is a boy— as does your Robbie—but whatever the Lord has planned, we will be thankful and happy."

"Papa always said, 'Wee lassies hold the wand that charms our lives.' My big brother serving in the Outer Hebrides is evidence of that kind of thinking. He is tough, strong, and brave, like Papa, but I am the one Papa says holds his heart."

Laughing softly, Lady Somerville said, "Och, it is true. Something about a wee lassie melts the heart of the strongest man."

The double oak doors of the solar opened abruptly, startling Katherine and Lady Somerville at the sudden entrance of Robbie, Katherine's tall and regal-looking husband.

Beaming broadly, he greeted Katherine and his mother with a kiss on the cheek. "Ah, Katherine, Mother, I see you two are hard at it. We are almost finished with the preparations and ready to place the flags along the route marking the race. Perhaps I will win this year, aye, Katherine?"

"This will be an interesting race—that is certain. And of course, Robbie, I do hope you win," said Katherine reaching for his hand.

"Well," Robbie said as he fondly kissed Katherine's hand, "I understand there is quite a lot of competition, but I will do my best to beat your determined cousin Peter." He turned to his mother. "Father is making the final arrangements for the feast, ordering baskets of food, and inviting everyone he meets. Be sure, we will have some surprise guests!"

Lady Somerville shook her head, a knowing smile curving her lips. "No doubt, cook will need some extra help if your father is inviting the entire county. He loves to entertain, as you well know; but on the occasion of the Red Hose Race and with royalty in attendance, the three days of feasting will surpass any previous feast day, if I know Sir Hugh."

"I must see to the final details of the guest rooms as well," Lady Somerville added. "Some guests will be staying over after the race for the hunting and hawking."

"I have organized the men for the butchering of the cattle, sheep, and game birds; so all is in readiness for the feast," Robbie added.

"Here are the red stockings for the winner"—Katherine held aloft a pair of brightly colored red woolen hose—"the prize for first place in the race, so I've done my part. I knitted them especially with you in mind, Robbie, so you better win, my love. Peter says he will beat you and wear these same red stockings during the feast."

"Ha! We will see about that," Robbie said good-naturedly. "However, I must tell you, I've seen him running around the village square more than once. I think he is hoping to win the red stockings for Jenny, just to show off, so he is getting in shape for the race. I almost hate to beat him, but . . . "

"May the fastest man win." Katherine laughed. "Peter is a few years younger than you, Robbie, so don't be so sure you will be wearing the red hose yourself."

"It probably won't be either of us; more's the pity for the barony," said Robbie, dropping a kiss on Katherine's forehead. "Many entries from the surrounding villages are registered this year." Robbie shook his head in wonder. "All this blather for a pair of red hose!"

"Aye, but it is so much fun." Katherine grinned.

"Of course, ye kin, it is a village tradition that hopefully will last for years to come. And of course, it is a great opportunity for our locals to make some extra coin," Robbie noted. "The vendors are setting up their booths even as we speak."

Chapter 8

And now abideth faith, hope, and charity . . . but the greatest of
these is charity.

1 Corinthians 13:13

SITTING NEXT TO KATHERINE ON the overstuffed sofa, Robbie circled her shoulders with one strong arm. "Are you feeling well, Katherine?" With his free hand, he turned her face to look at him, placing his cool hand against her soft cheek. "Not long now, my love, until you go into confinement, aye?" A worried look crossed his brow, and he said, "Thankfully, it won't be until after the race and all the guests have gone home. We certainly do not want a house full of visitors with a baby coming."

"I am doing well, Robbie," Katherine said, laughing softly while covering his hand with her own. "I be just fine, as Papa would say. All our old friends and guests will be here for the Red Hose Race—like a clan gathering of sorts—and I am so excited. After the race and the feasting, everyone will leave for their homes by the time I am ready for confinement. Och, my love, what an awful word! Confinement— like prison. Whoever thought this up?"

Robbie chuckled, shaking his head. "Nay, I am not looking forward to your confinement, that is certain. I can hardly bear being away from you, not even for one night. But, aye, this is my first babe, and I want to follow the confinement rules so all will happen as it should." He sighed, his eyes searching hers. "When you had wee John, I know you had a difficult time, so that makes me somewhat fearful. I could not bear to lose you, Katherine."

"Do not fear, Robbie. Dinna fash yourself, my love. Wee John was my first bairn, and I was so distressed at the time. No family was with me. I felt so alone and frightened. I asked Jamie if Lady Somerville could be with me, but he refused. Jamie was not with me either, as is the custom. He came later. He could not abide the births of any of his children."

"I want to be with you, Katherine. I am your husband, the babe's father."

Katherine looked at him lovingly. "I am afraid that is not possible. Women only, ye kin. But, my love, this time is different. You are here, Robbie; your mother is here with skilled midwives at the ready. I feel very comfortable and restful. Please do not worry. All is well."

Lady Somerville raised her eyebrows. She could not help overhearing the conversation. "Well, children," said Lady Somerville, addressing her son and daughter-in-law, "all will be well." She wanted to change the subject from the ongoing concerns over the coming birth of Robbie's first babe and what might happen. Her mind went to Katherine's own mother, who had died in childbirth.

"I have heard that the magistrates are planning to attend the Red Hose Race as well," she said pausing in her knitting. "Some coming from far away as Saint Andrews, so I am told. Surely, they are not just coming for the race. This event would be of no interest to them. The magistrates always going about the village worries me. Have you any news of this, Robbie?"

"Dear Lady Mother, you know they are always hanging around our gatherings, spying and nosing about as usual. Of late, Peter has been seen with men who have been said to be planning an uprising against papal tyranny, but there is no proof. It is all just speculation and idle blather."

"The believers must be careful all the same," said Katherine. "Peter is getting bolder, and I do pray he is not—as you say—plotting an uprising here in Lanarkshire. Since David Beaton took control at Saint Andrews, I have noticed an increase in the number of magistrates patrolling the area."

"Aye, we must be careful," Robbie agreed. "But let us not think of those friends and neighbors held in prison, those awaiting inquest. We pray daily for them. That is all we can do." He sighed. "Living these many years facing oppression and cruel tyranny in our land will dampen our spirits. Och, lassie, this is not the time to worry over magistrates. We want to have a merry time at the race and the festivities afterward, aye?"

"Indeed, my love," Katherine said as she laid a hand against his cheek.

She looked long into her husband's hazel eyes, remembering how Robbie Somerville had loved her and had waited for her during the long years she was at court. Then, after her release from the king's summons, they had worked their way through the pain and hurt of Katherine's compliance with the royal order. It was not easy; but with God's guidance, they had found their way back to each other. Remarkably enough, they had married with the king's blessing.

When James V of Scotland had granted permission for Katherine to return to private life under her father's protection, his heart was broken. He could never marry the lass, for she was not of royal blood; but even so, he wanted her to be happy. He would marry Marie de Guise, the political alliance chosen for him, so he sent Katherine away with his blessing, to the man she truly loved—Robbie Somerville.

Jamie's last words to Katherine before releasing her from court had been, "Remember this, Katherine—my dear, sweet Katherine— every time I breathe, I will think of you. Ye have called it madness— this love I have for you—but know this: I have learned to love, to care, by loving you. Do not forget me."

Chapter 9

For the arms of the wicked shall be broken:
but the LORD upholdeth the righteous.

Psalm 37:17

POPE PAUL III, SUPREME AUTHORITY over the Holy Mother Church of Rome, appointed Archbishop David Beaton as a cardinal. The office was to act as an advisor to the pope along with other ordained cardinals, who served as administrators of the Church of Rome.

His appointment was bad news for the Christian believers of the New Testament who opposed the dictatorial rule of the pope of Rome and the non-biblical decrees required by the priests to gain Heaven. The persecution of the believers was ongoing, increasing steadily in the shires of Scotland.

The newly appointed Cardinal David Beaton was ruthless and brutal, hunting down and burning all who defied his authority and casting into prison any who had a New Testament in their possession or even talked of the great enlightenment sweeping across the southern borders into Scotland.

As cardinal for the pope and archbishop over the parish of Saint Andrews, Beaton was one of James V's most trusted advisers; and it was largely due to the archbishop's influence that James became more closely aligned to France and more alienated from his uncle, Henry VIII of England.

Because of his brutality and keeping of a mistress who bore him a brood of illegitimate children, Cardinal David Beaton was not widely revered by most Scots. Much of his power and patronage was gained by way of his uncle and predecessor at Saint Andrews, James Beaton, a man of great influence and a former archbishop who vigorously sought the chancellorship of Scotland.

But James Beaton's most heinous act as archbishop was to burn young Patrick Hamilton to the stake for heresy. Hamilton was a well-beloved Scottish Reformer, whose only crime was to preach from the English New Testament. Having received scathing reprimands from the Scottish Reformers and the public in general, James Beaton was only too happy to pass the appointment as archbishop of Saint Andrews to his nephew.

The present archbishop of Saint Andrews and newly appointed cardinal, David Beaton held no reservations about using the great wealth of the Holy Mother Church and stipends from His Holiness, the pope, to enrich his own coffers and his own family. His personal life was not founded on biblical principles of morality; and he soon came to personify everything that was greedy, cruel, corrupt, and immoral in the ruling Church of Scotland.

David Beaton sat leisurely in an ornately carved chair in his private study. A designated courier placed in his hand a packet of money enclosed in parchment paper. Beaton leaned back in his chair while the courier watched him eagerly count the French currency. A slow smile spread across the archbishop's angular features.

David Beaton was a tall, lanky man with loose-fitting joints. His complexion was swarthy, his face narrow and thin. A pointed brown beard covered his chin, and his dark eyes were shrewd and calculating and reflected little warmth.

He dismissed the French courier and handed the packet of money to his assistant, who added it to a large wooden chest bolted to a shelf on the wall. His assistant unlocked the chest and placed the money on top of an overflowing mound of coins and official-looking documents and drafts. He then relocked the chest and handed the key to Beaton.

By favor of his predecessor, his uncle, James Beaton, Archbishop of Glasgow, David Beaton was granted this prominent position at Saint Andrews. For this lucrative political and spiritual post, he collected an annual revenue of ten thousand livres—a huge income for an archbishop. This stipend from France was only a portion of monies he received from the Scottish coffers and from nobles and tenants in his bishopric. He was also granted properties and lands amounting to a sizable fortune.

After he negotiated the marriage of King James V with Marie de Guise of France and for his close connections to King Francis I, Pope Paul III made Beaton a cardinal, a position that included this annual stipend of money from the Holy Mother Church at Rome. He was just forty-four years old and at the height of his ambitions.

Despite his vow of celibacy as an ordained priest of the Holy Catholic Church of Rome, Beaton kept a mistress, Marion Ogilvy, who bore him eight children, each of whom he appointed to lucrative positions by virtue of his position as cardinal. He also fathered over twenty illegitimate children by other mistresses. This double standard of priestly misconduct did not sit well with the people of Scotland.

Those who demanded accountability of their priests and requested moral reform in the Church were quickly silenced by the persuasive authority of the powerful Roman hierarchy. Many lost their lands; their positions and businesses were seized; their names were blacklisted, making it difficult to find other positions or trades. To question the infallibility and moral soundness of the priesthood was cause for inquest and punishment.

The fear of excommunication, years in purgatory, and eternal damnation kept many a mouth shut tight. But there were some who emerged from this darkness, some who dared to challenge the authority of the pope and his tyrannical power and the Church's authority to determine the fate of man's soul.

"You may go now," Beaton said to his assistant in a commanding tone, "but find Lady Marion and ask her to meet me in the conference room. See that we are not disturbed."

"As you wish, Your Holiness," the assistant said with a nod. He backed from the room in deference to royal custom and went in search of the cardinal's mistress.

In a matter of minutes, the door opened; and Lady Marion Ogilvy, a dark-haired woman in her late thirties, entered the large conference room where Archbishop Beaton conducted his business.

"Come, sit," he said pointing to the chair next to him. "I have something to say that might interest you, and I would like your opinion, your view on the matter."

"I am flattered, my lord," she said seating herself close to him and smiling. "I am always at your disposal, as you know." She cast a sly glance at the widely feared archbishop, who smiled sardonically at his long-time mistress. "How can I be of service, my lord?"

Lady Marion Ogilvy was considered by many to be a charming beauty, whose vast wealth and noble birth made her a sought-after asset for a marriage contract. She was the daughter of James Ogilvy, Lord Ogilvy I of Airlie, lord of the family estate in Angus. Both her parents were deceased, and she had become an heiress of the family estate. Beaton was a master at manipulation and soon had the young heiress in his control.

At the time of her parents' death, Lady Marion met David Beaton, Abbot of Arbroath Abbey. They had formed a close friendship; and because Marion owned a large estate and was still unmarried, Beaton had pursued a romantic relationship with her. Beaton could not marry her because of his vows of celibacy; so the two simply lived together at Ethie Castle, a nearby sandstone keep built by the monks at Arbroath Abbey.

The churchmen of Rome simply winked at this arrangement. After all, they reasoned, he had not married; his relationship with Marion was merely for carnal purposes; and his personal life was his business. Any who challenged the hypocrisy of the priesthood were threatened with excommunication, which resulted in eternal damnation. This fear held the people of Scotland in bondage and spiritual oppression.

"Aye, Marion, I have received a considerable sum of money from France, my annual stipend for my services at Saint Andrews," announced Cardinal Beaton, pointing to the money chest bolted to the library shelf.

"That is a good thing, is it not?" Marion queried. "I am pleased to hear that France has been so generous with you." She took his hand in hers and smiled happily at his good fortune.

"In addition," continued the cardinal, "the pope is rewarding me for arranging the marriage of Marie de Guise, a devout Catholic of noble birth, to our young King James, thereby strengthening our allegiance with France."

He tapped his fingers lightly on the mahogany desk, smiling to himself over accomplishing this alliance with Catholic France; and by doing so, he gained power and influence in his native Scotland. *I will rise even higher when I stamp out the rebel rousers, this protestant heresy,* he mused.

"Wonderful news, my lord! France is a strong ally for all of Scotland. You must be very pleased." Marion furrowed her brow, not sure why he was recounting to her his recent accomplishments.

"However, Marion, we are still facing a contingent of rebels who are constantly raising up to denounce the rights of the Church of Rome to act as the religious authority for their lives." Beaton unconsciously rubbed his temples in frustration. "This threat to my supreme power in Scotland must be stopped, I say. Haven't I been appointed cardinal by the pope?"

"Och, my lord, last year, those two Dominican friars were put to death in Stirlingshire—the two Johns, Keillor and Beveridge—and that nasty burning set off further rebellion. You must be careful, my dear. I hate the thought of heretic trials, anyway. Let them believe whatever they choose." She brushed back a stray lock of hair, shaking her head slightly. "And what did they do to deserve a death on the pyre?"

"Marion," he said sounding incredulous, "they had in their possession Tyndale's English translation of the New Testament and alleged this was the true Word of God. They discounted the edicts of our father, the pope, and his authority claiming the decrees of the

Church were not contained in Tyndale's translation. How could you not know this?"

Marion blanched at his words. "Of course," Marion reasoned, "all Scots who can read will find a smuggled copy of that forbidden text. But honestly, David, what harm can that do? That law against owning or reading the English translation only make them want to read it—and more so."

"Exactly, so we will know who the heretics are, the friars and the traitor churchmen, those who refuse to recant for breaking the law. They will be punished by the law, burned on Castle Hill at Edinburgh like common criminals," Beaton said coldly.

"Frankly, I am sorry to hear of these heretic deaths," Marion said. "But, my dear, this is no fault of yours—not completely. The council confirmed your decisions and condemned them as defiant and unrepentant; but I must say, it worries me. There are always repercussions." She paused and drew in a deep breath. "Of course, my dear, you are not to blame."

"Och, Marion, I do not blame myself. Quite the contrary, I would that every heretic was silenced or made to recant. That is why the council listens to my judgment. They have yet to oppose me, and I never grant a pardon unless a substantial bribe is offered."

A frown creased Marion's forehead. "I don't understand why money can stop an execution if the person were guilty."

The archbishop's eyes grew hard as granite, and he glared at Marion with irritation. "We need the money to fight the dissenters, Marion. Their resolute stand only incites more to join their ranks against the Church. And despite our efforts to stop them, their numbers grow. They are multiplying like rabbits."

"But surely, if enough so-called heretics face the inquisitors and spend time in those horrible dungeons, they will think twice before refusing to recant," Marion suggested.

"I do not think you understand, my dear. Those measures only seem to strengthen their resolve. I must find a way to stop them. I am thinking of using this money to hire spies, infiltrate the most suspicious of their ranks. Money talks, ye kin?" he said, smiling cynically.

"Aye, it does. How well we both know this," she said ruefully.

Marion turned away to look out the window, her mind going to her own vast wealth and how it purchased many things, loyalty included. The thought was disconcerting.

"Reports come to me of a Reformation Rider, as he is called," the cardinal said, "and the word is that he has been seen in the Lanarkshire region of the border country. He is the one suspected of rescuing condemned heretics at the very point of certain death. So far, he has escaped without a trace. He must have powerful friends that aid him and protect him from discovery. We will find these friends and pay them handsomely for information to his identity."

"I am not personally acquainted with the families of the border regions," Marion said, "but I hear from time to time of their gatherings, of marriages and legacies of lands and titles. Such matters are of interest to everyone. Many of their sympathies are known but not challenged. There is much hearsay among the nobles and landowners, of course."

"We must find more than hearsay," Cardinal Beaton said, scowling. "My informants tell me there is a race in the parish of Carnwath, in the region of the Valley of the Clyde—the Red Hose Race they call it, a well-known event with many in attendance. A gathering such as that is the perfect place to send spies to gather information and discover their secret meeting places. We know these so-called believers meet; but they change locations, so we can't catch them."

"That sounds like an excellent idea," Marion said encouragingly. "There is always an exchange of conversation and the latest gossip at such events. I believe you are on the right track for finding intelligence on the heretics, those who oppose the Holy Mother Church."

"That is exactly what I needed to hear, my dear—that my plan to root out those trouble making rebels is a possible way to pursue the enemies of the Church. I will send my best spies to the Red Hose Race to learn all they can about the Lowland clans with enough money to make them talk, aye, Marion?"

"But I urge you, David, the burnings are too harsh of punishment for simply having a Bible translated into English. Find a less cruel way of causing the heretics to repent and recant of their misguided ways."

David Beaton looked at his long-time consort. He smiled slyly at her soft, womanly suggestion, but he said nothing. In his heart, he knew the dire effects that little books would have on his own power if the people discovered that the long-reigning religious traditions of Rome were challenged and exposed as false. Already, that small, cheaply bound book was making inroads into Scotland, and he must stop the Reformers and their preaching from that book.

He nodded to Marion as though considering her request, but his swarthy features reflected a perverse satisfaction in his clever plan to rid Scotland of this ongoing Reformation lunacy once and for all. He had the power and the money, the vital means to stop this madness.

In the Scottish Highlands, the religious Reformation of Europe and England had not yet reached to the Isles and outer regions of Scotland. The landscape was formidable, and the people untaught in the Scriptures. The mass was spoken in Latin, so they relied on the parish priest to absolve their sins and get them to Heaven. Ignorance of God's Divine Word was the controlling influence.

But in the Lowlands and border regions with proximity to England and Europe, copies of the English Bible were smuggled across the borders by daring Reformers. The Scriptures written in their own language set off a wave of religious zeal among the people.

But the archbishops and cardinals of the Roman Church, who for a thousand years had controlled the people through fear and intimidation, were determined to find a way to stamp out this Reformation movement through Romish heretic trials.

Chapter 10

I returned, and saw under the sun, that the race is not to the swift,
nor the battle to the strong, neither yet bread to the wise . . .
but time and chance happeneth to them all.
Ecclesiastes 9:11

THE MORNING MIST ROSE SLOWLY, drifting across the Valley of the Clyde and bathing the hills with drops of flower-scented vapor. In the woodlands, bluebells, swaying in the warm breeze like dancers in perfect rhythm, carpeted the forest floors. After the mist faded away, the day promised to be a pleasant day for the inhabitants of Clyde Valley.

In the village of Carnwath, flags were placed along the five-mile racing course, local roads chosen for their obstacles. The villagers dug trenches, filled them with water, and placed sizeable logs and brush along the racetrack to make the race more exciting and to test the endurance and determination of the runners. The winner of the Red Hose Race would receive a monetary award as part of the prize, and the young men from the surrounding villages were enthusiastic, all hoping to win.

The Carmichaels were guests of the Somervilles at Cowthally Castle. They were eager to visit with Katherine and wee Johnny and, of course, to watch the Red Hose Competition with Peter and Robbie vying for the prize. Sir John and William waited for Sir Hugh to join them for a light breakfast already laid out on a hunting buffet in the sunny upper solar.

A fire burned brightly on the stone hearth and lit the corners of the smaller room with a golden glow. The solar, an informal area for entertaining—a place where folks could let down their hair, talk, laugh, and play games and music—was used by the women folk for sewing and stitching. Tapestries hung over inlaid wood panels, and a bank of windows faced the south wall, allowing for light and warmth in the winter months. It was a lovely room, private and welcoming.

"I understand, William, that Lorna Forrest and her parents are coming for the race," Sir John said, addressing his brother who was staring out the windows as though watching for someone. A smile curving his lips, William turned to Sir John.

"Aye, they should be here soon," William said. "I am thinking it be time for ye to know I am fond of the lass, John. Lorna has never married and is younger than meself, quite a few years. After her brother was martyred, she remained with her parents, devoted to them, more so after her brother was executed at Saint Andrews."

"Commendable of the lass," remarked Sir John, "to care for her grieving parents, aye, indeed. Ye have talked of them so often after your visits to the stables at Linlithgow; so naturally, I assumed there might be more going on than simply overseeing the king's horses, aye, William?"

William paused, wondering if his older brother, the clan chief who depended on him to watch over the lands of Carmichael, might not be pleased with his growing affection for the lass. "Do ye object to my interest in Lorna, John?"

"Quite the contrary," said Sir John, a serious tone to his voice. "Ye have spent too many years grieving over Maggie. Aye, and turned ye into a solitary man, a man who would do well with the tender love of a woman. May not be the same as when ye loved Maggie, but ye can be a man who can love again—and be happy again. Ye be blessed to find another to love in your one lifetime if that be God's will."

William studied his indomitable brother, a man who was almost like a father to him. He knew Sir John to be wise to carefully consider the needs of his people and the outcome of every decision, and this shrewd sagacity had won him a knighthood. In battle, he was a leader, a force to be reckoned with. But in peacetime, he was a gentle, kind, and caring clan chief.

"And what of ye, me chieftain brother?" queried William. "Have ye no desire to wed again?"

A slow smile crinkled the lines around Sir John's eyes, and he sipped his glass of cider before answering. His voice was low, gravelly, and edged with a touch of sadness.

"Ye know how I loved Gwendolyn. A rare treasure, she was. I do not grieve, William. So long ago now and I be old, full of years." He paused, taking a deep breath before continuing. "Memories of those days with Gwendolyn are like opening a treasure box of precious gems in my life. But nay, I be content, satisfied with God's plan."

Assured of a life well-lived, Sir John smiled. "God knows if our destiny be meant for only one. Me years with Gwennie . . . aye, it was enough to last me lifetime, but not all men feel the same. Not everyone be content."

"Aye, I understand. I thought never to wed again meself, to put the thought of another lass far from me heart; but on the way home from that last rescue of the heretic priest, I found a glass bottle in the heather. Ye know, John, God puts our tears in a bottle[7] and remembers our grief. He not only remembers, but He also bottles them up."

"Aye, He does that," Sir John agreed. He remembered with a thread of sadness his young wife—the sweetness and gentleness she had brought to his rough soldier's life. Gwendolyn had warmed his heart with her caring ways. Even now, after so many years, he could feel her deep sorrow when they had laid their two infant sons in the tiny graves on Kirk Hill. Aye, he had known sorrow, but he had also known love.

"I did that, too, John, like God does for us. I bottled up my grief for Maggie—the memories. I understood that long ago, I knew love and it was good."

"Ye kin, William, the wise man said, 'Many waters cannot quench love, neither can the floods drown it: if a man would give all the substance of his house for love, it would utterly be contemned.'"[8]

"Aye, John, ye kin . . . so it is true, and ye are to be admired for being happy with your one love."

Hoping for this private moment with his brother before Sir Hugh arrived at the solar, William pushed his chair close to John.

"After that last rescue," William continued in a low voice, "traveling home to Carmichael, somehow, the bottle seemed significant, like God was saying, 'It be time to bottle up your tears. It be time to make memories.' Perhaps, if God wills, with another lass."

---

7   Psalm 56:8
8   Song of Solomon 8:7

Sir John laughed softly, his blue eyes twinkling at his brother's words. "Me thinks, lad, ye best keep that bottle close where ye can remember that the past is bottled up, like a wee glass memorial. God is speaking to ye, I believe."

"That be true, John. Being with Lorna quiets me spirit. Hard to explain how me heart has softened and feels warm again after years of coldness, but Lorna melts the cold places and fills an empty place in me heart. And it seems . . . aye, the time seems right."

The door to the solar opened with a whoosh; and Sir Hugh entered with a flourish, ending the brother's discussion, "Getting ready to start the race soon, so best we hurry, me friends. Ye should find the best place to cheer on the lads! The race starts at the east end of the village and, after the five-mile endurance, will end at the Mercat Cross at the town center. I will be there to present the prize."

Sir Hugh turned to William. "Och, lad, ye have guests waiting for ye at the front entrance." He smiled and winked at Sir John. Sir Hugh was a pleasant man with round, amicable features, curly white hair, hazel eyes, and a generous heart.

The three men left the solar and hurried down the wide stairway to the front entrance where Thomas and Iyla Forrest waited for William. Lorna was not with her parents, and William felt a keen disappointment as he greeted his friends.

"Sir Hugh, Sir John, this is Thomas and Iyla Forrest," said William, "the family I have often spoken of when I am at Linlithgow stables." After the introductions were exchanged, the two men left William to escort the visitors to the location where servants had planned an observation area for the Somervilles and their company of visitors to watch the race.

Chapter 11

But none of these things move me, neither count I my life dear unto myself, so that I might finish my course with joy.

Acts 20:24

IN NO TIME, SIR JOHN and Sir Hugh were lost amid the gathering crowd vying for an advantageous position to watch the Red Hose Race. It appeared that the entire county had turned out for the event. Vendors, hoping for a profitable day for selling their goods, set up booths and tents along the roadway.

"I see Lorna is not with ye. Is she not coming for the race?" William queried as Thomas and Iyla walked with him at a more leisurely pace.

"Och, William, "she is here," Iyla said, smiling. "Your host, Lady Somerville, grabbed her away from us when we left the carriage. She wanted to show Lorna around and take her to the race with her ladies. I understand your niece is expecting soon and will not be with the rest of us, so Lady Somerville took her to meet Katherine. How kind of her."

"Aye, she is a kind and caring woman," agreed William. "She mentored Katherine during her growing-up years, and Katherine often spent the summer months at Cowthally Castle under her guidance and protection."

They approached the designated course, where people from the surrounding villages were lining the road where the race would soon begin. Sir John waved a hand above the crowd when he saw William with Thomas and Iyla. They soon joined the rest of the Somerville company who were laughing and joking and making predictions on who would win the race.

Lorna was there, seated with Lady Somerville and her ladies. Peter and Robbie were there, too, dressed in their clan colors, a sash bearing their clan motto across one shoulder. They jostled and teased the waiting contestants now assembling at the starting line. Spirits were high, ready for the race to begin.

"The Fiery Dragon will win the red hose!" shouted Robbie Somerville, laughing and elbowing the nearest runner. "'Fear God in life,'" he called to the crowd, quoting the Somerville motto amid the din of whistles and laughter.

"Ha! Ye are daft, me friend," Peter cried above the cheers of the crowd. "The Men of the Broken Spear are *real* men, not mythical dragons that no person has ever seen. And not only that, but we are ever ready!"

As the eager crowd waited for the race to begin, a contingent of magistrates dressed in the king's royal livery positioned themselves along the route marked off for the race. Some were on horseback; and some were on foot, milling about, mixing with the assembled onlookers lined up along the racetrack. Going from booth to booth, they spoke to the vendors selling merchandise and tokens of the Red Hose Race.

Immediately, Sir John and William Carmichael were on alert. They carried their weapons but rarely had cause to use them. They expected magistrates to be present, like they were at every local event, but not in such great numbers. The magistrate scanned the crowd as though searching for a particular person. Noting one of the officers looking their way, Sir John spoke quietly to William, who moved silently away and melted among the crowd of spectators.

Had the king ordered this large contingent of magistrates? Sir John wondered. More than likely, it would be the wily Archbishop David Beaton, who waited with bated breath for his spies to find an opportunity to discover the meeting places of the secret believers, those who had never conformed to the Romish Church dictates or who spoke against the doctrines that held men in bondage and fear.

Large public gatherings, such as the Red Hose Race in the southern uplands of Lanarkshire, provided an opportunity to offer bribes for information. Money talked, loosening the tongues of any who knew the whereabouts of those who rebelled against papal authority. For years, the Reformation Rider had escaped discovery; but David Beaton was determined to capture him alive.

A huge red flag was dropped in place, marking the start of the race. The runners sprang forward, and the crowd erupted in shouts and applause. But like the drawing back of a bow string, tension slowly permeated the atmosphere; and the crowd watching the race grew restless, uncomfortable at the sight of so many royal officers scrutinizing them. There were too many incidents of arrests and interrogations for the people of the Clyde Valley not to fear the governing political and spiritual powers that ruled their land.

William strolled casually toward the area where Lorna sat with Lady Somerville and her guests. With a nod of his head, he beckoned to Lorna; and she excused herself from the group of ladies to meet him near an obscured stand of trees, a short distance from prying eyes. William had tethered his horse, Shadow, among the trees. The horse was munching on some grass; but at their approach, he lifted his head and whinnied.

"I must leave now, Lorna," said William quietly. "Sir John says to make myself invisible to this regiment of blood thirsty magistrates. It be obvious they are questioning the crowd, searching for someone to arrest. Stay close to the Somervilles, and then you and your parents return to Carmichael with Sir John when the race is over. I have a bad feeling and fear this will be a nasty business before this day is over."

Lorna's eyes widened, worry wrinkling her brow. "But, William, you haven't done anything to arouse their suspicion. If they see you leave so suddenly, won't they suspect you are guilty of something?"

"Ye kin, Lorna, the inquisitors at Saint Andrews have suspected me for some time, but they can never prove anything." He spoke quietly, his voice a mere whisper. "It matters little what I do at this point. Always in me mind, I feared this day would come; and it is no surprise." William sighed deeply, his frustration evident. Smiling almost shyly, he took Lorna's hand and kissed it softly,

"If they are truly after me today," said William, "I don't want them thinking we are together, endangering your family because of me. Thomas and Iyla have suffered enough loss." His eyes quickly scanned the wood as he looked for anything unusual.

"Please, Lorna, hurry back to Lady Sommerville and her ladies and then return to Carmichael with Sir John and your parents after the feast at Cowthally. Please, mind me words, Lorna."

Tears filled her eyes as she gently squeezed William's hand before grudgingly turning to leave. Living with the constant threat of arrest was wearing on her. Only last week, the magistrates had searched their home, inspecting the still room where she kept her herbal remedies; but they did not remark on the common garden herbs most folk kept for cooking and natural cures. She had not told William of this incident, for she did not wish to spoil the day for the rest of their company.

"Where will you go, William? Will you return to Carmichael?"

"Aye, lass, for now. Sir John will assess the reason for all the magistrates present today. I will meet you at Carmichael after the festivities at Cowthally Castle. Stay close to our people."

"I will, William," she promised. Reluctantly, she turned to leave the wood but saw Sir John approaching the clearing. Slipping away quietly, she hid herself behind a thick tangle of brushes. She waited to hear what Sir John would say to William.

Running lightly, Sir John approached the wood as William gathered Shadow's reins and prepared to mount.

"William!" shouted Sir John reaching his brother and grabbing Shadow's reins. He had come swiftly to warn him of an impending arrest of believers suspected of aiding and abetting the Reformation Rider. But Sir John was too late.

Suddenly, a contingent of royal guards and magistrates dressed for battle broke from the wood where they had been hiding. Their horses thundering, dust flying in the morning air, they surrounded William with their swords drawn, their battle axes at the ready.

Pointing a sword at William's chest, the chief officer bellowed in a loud voice so that all could hear. "Are ye William Carmichael of Carmichael?" he questioned, then paused, and waited for William to answer. The magistrate's swarthy face wore a triumphant smirk looking around at his fellow officers. But William answered nothing.

"If so—if ye are William Carmichael of Carmichael, the so-called Reformation Rider—then ye are under arrest on the charge of heresy and treason on orders from the king of Scotland and His Holiness, the pope, and the Holy Mother Church of Rome. Hand over your weapons at once and do not try to escape, or ye will be cut down."

Instinctively, William reached for his sword; but he felt the tight grip of Sir John's strong hand squeezing his sword arm, thwarting his attempt to fight his way out. "Do as they say, William," said Sir John in his low, gravelly voice. "This is not the time to fight. There be too many."

Several of the guards held William, roughly pinning his arms and searching his person for hidden weapons. Next, they tied his hands in front of him with rough hemp bindings to prevent any further reaction from their captive. William refused to answer any questions; and for his refusal, he was violently struck across the face, splitting his skin open with a bloody wound. On finding a dirk in his boot, they punched him in the ribs. Still, William said nothing.

Sir John tried reasoning with the guard but to no avail. William nodded to his brother, a silent warning to stay out of the questioning, lest they also accuse him.

The guard forcefully pushed William toward his mount, causing him to stumble to the ground. They lifted him to his feet and then to his own mount; but Shadow, his faithful horse, sensed trouble and would have none of it. He reared; and pawing the air, he unseated William, whose hands were tied. Unable to steady himself, William spoke to Shadow, settling his mount so he could stay in the saddle.

A short distance from the wood, now swarming with soldiers and magistrates, Lorna stayed hidden among the brush and watched the outcome of the altercation with the king's men. In just moments,

William sat astride his horse, hands tied, weapons gone, his bloodied face a study of defiance. Surrounding the captive, the royal guard was moving away from the wood, determined to deliver William, the suspected Reformation Rider, to Edinburg without further incident.

Chapter 12

And fear not them which kill the body, but are not able to kill the soul:
but rather fear him which is able to destroy both soul and body in hell.

Matthew 10:28

"THE MAGISTRATES . . . " Lorna gasped as she reached the area where
the Somerville ladies were seated on a grassy bank near the roadway
watching the race from this gentle slope.

The collective ladies group looked up in surprise and noted with
some alarm Lorna's disheveled appearance and her tremulous voice.
Her breath was coming in near sobs. She had hurriedly left the wood
when William was being questioned by the magistrates.

"They have taken William," continued Lorna, her voice breaking.
"I hid myself in the shelter of the trees to hear what the magistrates
said. William was arrested on a charge of heresy and treason."

Rising to her feet at Lorna's breathless demeanor, Lady Somerville
said, "What did you say?" The group of women seated on a bank rose
with Lady Somerville, a sense of outrage and indignation moving
swiftly among them at Lorna's announcement.

"A charge of treason, you say," queried Lady Somerville in
astonishment. "How can this be and where?" Catching her breath,
she cast an intense gaze at Lorna's trembling form now quivering in

fear. "Where were Sir John, Lorna, and his men while this trouble is going on?"

"I left the immediate area quickly when I realized what was happening," Lorna said, wringing her hands. "The men and Sir John were talking with the magistrates, said they had orders from the king of Scotland and His Holiness, the pope, and the Holy Mother Church of Rome." Tears welled up in her eyes, and she quickly wiped them away with the back of her hand.

"Then," she said, her words faltering as she spoke, "they took William's weapons, tied his hands, and set him on his horse, abusing him with their fists as they did so. He was bleeding from a cut on his face. I heard Sir John caution him to be compliant and not resist. Then the guard left the wood with haste, avoiding the spectators. Riding for Edinburgh, I believe they said."

"Orders from the king of Scots!" Lady Somerville said, while gathering her entourage in preparation to leave for Cowthally Castle. "We shall see about that! The young king and his new wife are our guests, so I highly doubt if Jamie ordered William's arrest."

At her words, Lorna began to hope. "Come now, dear Lorna. I know you lost your brother to the inquisition, which is bound to be upsetting at this news. But never fear; God will help us sort this out."

"But, dear lady," Lorna said, hot tears streaming down her pale face, "William was there when Henry was martyred, watching the execution after failure to rescue him. And now, they have taken him, too. Oh, Lady Somerville, it is still too raw, too dreadful to think William will meet the same fate."

"Nay, nay, sweet girl," encouraged Lady Somerville, "we have some influence with the king, as do the Men of the Broken Spear, Clan

Carmichael. The young king spent much time in the parish of Camwath pursuing Katherine; and I assure you, I did my best to stop that young profligate. I am not afraid to take on His High-and-Mightiness."

"But they have introduced laws that will condemn any who oppose the Church of Rome," Lorna said as she gathered up her cloak and gloves.

"Aye, indeed, they have done so; but God knows the loopholes in the law, so don't despair. Besides, they dare not take on all of Lanarkshire, its clan chiefs, and lords over one man who assists the believers. It must be proven. Let us go and see what must be done."

On the return of the ladies to Cowthally Castle, Lady Somerville quickly took charge of the household, ordering the grooms to house the carriages and groom the horses and for the cooks to begin to prepare food for the soon-returning guests. This would be a long night for the Men of the Broken Spear planning a strategy for the unexpected arrest of their neighbor and friend.

Sir Hugh stayed behind at the village to watch the outcome of the race. He was unaware that William had been taken prisoner by the royal guard and was now on the road to Edinburgh to face charges of treason and heresy. Not wanting the crowd to observe the arrest of William Carmichael, the arresting magistrates followed a partly wooded trail away from the racing track.

Meanwhile, the five-mile cross country race continued amid cheers and shouts of the crowd with Peter and Robbie now in the lead. On the last leg of the race that ended at the Mercat Cross at the center of the village, Robbie tripped over a pile of brush in the roadway and fell headlong into a trough of water. He saw Peter glance over his shoulder and laugh. Two young lads from Biggar sprinted around him, also laughing as they ran past.

Dripping and muddy, Robbie moved to the side of the road just as two more racers leaped over the brush to land in the same slippery water trough. The spectators cheered wildly as the two water-soaked contestants joined Robbie on the roadside amid gales of laughter. This was great entertainment for the bystanders who purposely chose this vantage point in hopes of seeing the racers hit the water.

Sir Hugh waited at the Mercat Cross to present the winner with the coveted pair of red hose and the purse of money. The lords of Somerville had presided over this ceremony for years. It was a community tradition enjoyed by all of Lanarkshire since its beginning in 1508. At the outcome of the race, there would be a celebration at the Wee Bush Pub for any who cared to participate.

Genevieve Chancellor—Jenny to those who knew her—Peter's close friend, also waited at the Mercat Cross, praying that Peter would win the prize and wear the red hose to celebrate. She would not have long to wait. Peter came running in the lead with the two lads from Biggar close behind.

Shouts and hurrahs filled the air as Peter dashed across the finish line in first place. Flags waved, and the feet-stomping began. Peter saw Jenny jumping up and down, clapping and laughing, her auburn hair falling from her bonnet and her eyes sparkling with joy. He had won this race just for her. Wearing the coveted red hose and teasing the waterlogged Robbie Somerville, they would join the others at Cowthally Castle.

Peter had pursued friendship with Genevieve Chancellor after rescuing her from her abusive father. Because she was a minor at the time and under her father's authority, Sir John advised her to return to her home and father and submit herself to his authority while trying to establish a better relationship by showing love and kindness.

Jenny's smuggled copy of the New Testament in English was discovered in her possession by a servant, considered heresy by law; so after her father had punished her with a sound beating, she had fled from her father, who she felt would take her to the parish priest to confess and then possibly face a hearing and trial.

After Sir John's strong warning against reporting Jenny, Chancellor began to soften, allowing a "friendship" only between Peter and Jenny. But now, several years later, Jenny was of age; and she and Peter continued their relationship, which had grown much deeper.

Oddly enough, Edward Chancellor turned a blind eye. He kept the smuggled copy instead of turning it over to the parish priest, hiding it in a secret place in his library and locking the door. He intended to burn the Testament in the fireplace to remove any evidence of Jenny's rebellion.

The magistrates regularly searched the homes of sympathizers, those who might have copies of the English New Testament. But Edward Chancellor was not a sympathizer and had a son who served in a monastery off the coast of France, Mont Saint Michel. Chancellor continually supported the Holy Mother Church and all its edicts and orders.

Sir John's sharp warning of what might happen if he took Jenny to the priest to confess had caused Chancellor to think better of reporting Jenny's duplicity by owning a smuggled copy of Tyndale's translation of the New Testament in English. Jenny suspected that her father might be reading the outlawed copy himself, secretly, thus the locked library door.

Chapter 13

For he hath said, I will never leave thee nor forsake thee. So that we
may boldly say, The Lord is my helper, and I will not fear what man
shall do unto me.

Hebrews 13:5-6

BY LATE AFTERNOON, THE GUESTS of the Somervilles arrived at Cowthally Castle, eager to celebrate with the winner of the Red Hose Race. But after learning of William's arrest, the guests were considerably disturbed and even outraged by news of the arrest by the magistrates who constantly patrolled the area. Residents living near to the Valley of the Clyde were weary of the magistrates and their ongoing search for dissenters and those noncompliant with the dictates of the Holy Mother Church.

The arrest of William Carmichael for treason and heresy appeared to be based on circumstantial evidence, for no witness directly accused him. The outcome would be decided by the privy council that advised the present monarch and Archbishop Beaton in all matters of the law and of disloyalty to the king and the Church of Rome.

The men who comprised the privy council were outwardly loyal to the king and jealously guarded their positions for the personal gain it afforded. The duty of the council was to apply lawful judgment to the offender. Their decision was to be impartial and unbiased and in the interest of Scotland and the Mother Church of Rome. But all too often, the decisions were based on what would keep their seats on the privy council and in good favor with the pope of Rome.

Although the privy council would present a ruling based on their judgment, the king could reject the council's decision if it concerned Scottish law, but young King James V could not overrule the pope. The council was powerful and used intimidation and devious means to influence the young monarch when it was to their advantage.

The festivities enthusiastically planned by Sir Hugh would commence after the Red Hose Race, but a cloud of gloom hung over the crowd gathered for the three days of activities. The king and his bride were to arrive on the third day to take in the hawking and hunting with the Somerville clan hosting the event. The best rooms had been prepared for the king and his entourage, and the entire village was excited for the reigning monarch of Scotland to visit their parish.

Robbie Somerville and several local chiefs and their head men were encouraged by Sir Hugh to meet in the library at Cowthally Castle to discuss the events leading up to William's apprehension and what steps, if any, should be taken to contest the arrest. Sir John Carmichael would surely be the spokesman for his brother, and the clan chiefs would more than likely defer to his judgment.

When Lady Somerville returned to Cowthally Castle with the ladies, she ordered the servants to bring a large hunting table to the library to serve the men gathered there for the meeting. The ornately carved table was laden with cold meats, cheeses, fruits, and a variety of baked goods, along with cider, hot tea, and small ale.

After the Red Hose Race had ended and Peter learned of his father's arrest, he was furious and took no pleasure in his victory. He found Jenny waiting for him at the Mercat Cross and drew her aside.

"Jenny," he said breathing heavily, "have you heard of father's arrest?" Peter wiped sweat from his brow. "And did you see the magistrates taking him away?"

"Nay, Peter. I have been here at the Mercat Cross all along, at the finish line, waiting for you to win." Jenny's thick auburn hair was tied back at the nape of her neck, and her freckles had come to the surface in the warm spring sunshine. "I'm so very sorry, Peter. I know your victory is a wee bit offsetting after learning of your father's arrest. You look so angry, my love. Do you have a plan?"

"Och Jenny, I dinna think of this happening during the race. My mind was on the race and the following days of celebration at Cowthally Castle with you, never guessing what those wicked magistrates and their spies were planning. But, lass, I must leave at once to see what must be done to free father. Sir Hugh has called a meeting, so it might be best for you to return to Shieldhill until I know what Sir John says."

He looked long into Jenny's green eyes, his own shadowing with a myriad of emotions. He remembered the day, long ago now, when he had picked the auburn-haired girl from the heather after she had fallen from her pony and their friendship was born. The friendship grew into love, and the flame of that love still burned.

They were so young then; but now, young adults, they patiently waited for Jenny's father, Edward Chancellor, to grant them permission to marry. But he was a hard man, a devout papist, and refused his blessing.

"Please, Peter, let me come with you. We have already planned to be at Cowthally for the festivities. Papa has given permission for Lady Somerville to be my chaperon, so all is well. I want to be with you."

"Nay, sweet love, I am reasonably certain that the clans will ride to Edinburgh and demand father's release from this unwarranted arrest. I intend to ride with them."

Jenny's eyes brimmed with tears. "We both know, Peter, it will not be that easy. Your father has been involved in helping the believers for many years now, and someone has possibly betrayed him."

"If that be so, I will hunt down the betrayer and make him withdraw his accusations."

Fearing for what he was saying and for what he might do in his anger, Jenny took both Peter's hands in her own. She knew he was gathering a force together to defy the oppression and tyranny the pope held over the Scottish people, but it could not be done with mere human strength. It would take a miracle.

"Peter, listen to me." Jenny looked away and saw in the distance the magistrates in their shining steel helmets, their orange tunics moving among the people. She turned again to Peter. "I understand your anger and frustration, but, my love, do not let the worst of wicked men ruin the best in you. Put away your anger and let God have control of this situation."

Slowly, Peter shook his head. "I fear the best in me cannot continue to stand by and do nothing. When I was a lad, I dinna understand what kept father at his mission to spare the believers; but I do now. It is a passion, a burning to right the wrong, to open the eyes of the people of Scotland. It is not just anger, Jenny; it is more than that." Seeing the tears in Jenny's eyes, he sighed.

"Then, come, Jenny; find your father and tell him that despite the arrest, we still plan to be present at Cowthally Castle. And you will be under the protection of Lady Somerville. Still, he may want you home at Shieldhill, but I must go with or without you. Your father is not happy that we wish to marry—you know that—so naturally, he is against anything I do."

"Papa may not be happy, Peter; but I am happy, and that is what is important to both of us. I feel that someday, he will relent and let us marry."

Preparing to leave for Cowthally Castle to meet with his uncle, Sir John, and the neighboring clan chiefs, Peter discovered Edward Chancellor in the crowd of people not far from the Mercat Cross.

Jenny waved a hand in greeting toward her father, who threaded his way through the crowd to where the young couple stood among the crowd. A scowl creased his face as he glared at Peter.

"Aye, Papa," she said in greeting. "You do remember that Peter and I plan to attend the festivities at Cowthally Castle? Lady Somerville will be my chaperone while I am present."

"Things have changed, Genevieve," Chancellor said with a frown.

On hearing of William Carmichael's arrest, Edward Chancellor withdrew permission for Jenny to attend the festivities at Cowthally Castle. He would take Jenny home to Shieldhill with him that very day. The young couple acquiesced, another disappointment in the rocky journey that would free them to marry.

Edward Chancellor moved away, signaling for his servants to bring their horse and light carriage; but before the young couple parted, Peter drew Jenny aside and said, "I love you, Jenny Chancellor. At first, in silence and secret, and now, in difficult times, between the light and dark spaces of where we find ourselves, our enduring love. But always remember, sweet lass, you hold my heart."

Chapter 14

I have taught thee in the way of wisdom; I have led thee in the right paths.

Proverbs 4:11

THE CLAN CHIEFS AND HEAD men of the Valley of the Clyde were, for the most part, united in their views of how things were governed by the hierarchy of Rome with the exceptions of the border reivers who paid little attention to the governing powers and could easily change loyalties if threatened.

When those who desired to attend the gathering at Cowthally Castle were present in the library, Sir Hugh presided over the meeting and rehearsed the details of the arrest and capture of William Carmichael, now on his way to be questioned by the privy council in Edinburgh. He then turned the meeting over to Sir John Carmichael.

Sir John stood, his bearing commanding, his years as a soldier and clan chief marked by character lines on his rugged features. Heavy brows shadowed his blue eyes that, despite his somewhat austere demeanor, were wise and kind. His thick hair was peppered with silver and black, and he wore a closely cropped beard.

Sir John looked at the clansmen assembled in the library, assessing each man with a keen perception of his character. He knew whom he could trust, those who would not allow fear to rule their decisions and the outcome of what would follow his judgment on how to proceed. For years, the clans of the southern uplands had worked together to maintain peace among the clans and families of the valley, and doing so had been no easy task.

"Me advice to this gathering of neighbors and clansmen, me friends, is to wait for the king, who will arrive in two days in Carnwath and is a guest of the Somervilles here at Cowthally Castle. We have been acquainted with the king since his youth, aye; but after he began to rule Scotland at age sixteen as our sovereign, little opportunity has afforded me to speak to the king about political and spiritual matters, except for releasing Katherine from"—he paused, a flicker of pain crossing his features—"from her duties at court."

"Aye, Uncle," Peter said in an agitated tone, "what you say is true. But by the time the king arrives, my father will suffer bodily abuse; and who knows what else those merciless jailers at the tollbooth will do to him? Should we not move quickly and proceed to Edinburgh?"

Peter Carmichael—William's raven-haired, blue-eyed son, now in his mid-twenties and considered a man in his own right—felt the plan presented by his chieftain uncle must be challenged. He remembered with anguish the tortuous death of Patrick Hamilton, the young Reformer who dared to challenge the abuses of the Holy Mother Church. Serving as Patrick's groom, Peter was made to witness the execution, a horrific scene he would never forget.

Now, concern for his father's welfare was uppermost in his mind. After all, he was secretly following in his father's footsteps, warning the believers. However, unbeknownst to his father and uncle, Peter was gathering a contingent of likeminded Scots to plan a rising at

Saint Andrews to take over the stronghold of the hierarchy of Rome, the center for the Holy Mother Church in Scotland.

"The lad has a point, Sir John," said Cockburn. "And even when the king arrives, who can say if he will do anything to reverse the charges of treason and heresy?"

"Aye, Sir John," offered Laird Cunningham, Earl of Glencairn, "indeed, we must not wait on the king to decide William's fate. He will surely approve of the privy council's decision to bring William to trial. The king is still a bairn in wisdom, I wager, and is fearful of losing those hefty stipends from the Romish hierarchy. He depends on the coin he gathers from Rome and France."

"A point to consider," agreed Sir John, "once the questioning is over and a trial is scheduled. And I be sure that will be the case if the council is not satisfied with the hearing; the utmost caution must be taken if we expect to free William before the trial begins."

Peter stood, his voice rising in anger. "We must not wait, Uncle. Perhaps he will be tortured into confessing . . . anything to satisfy the council. It is a common enough practice—torture and abuse—a method used to make the prisoners recant."

Sir John turned to his nephew, his face hardening with reproof. "I believe you underestimate your father's courage, Peter. I realize the arrest is a serious matter, totally unexpected; but it was never beyond possibility. And ye, Peter, of all who are gathered here, know what I speak of."

Others meeting in the library spoke up, some for waiting until the king's arrival and some for gathering a contingent of landowners and clansmen to go in force to Edinburgh. The privy council was wary of a united effort of lowland clansmen to challenge their authority. Powerful warriors, men of steel, determined in their purpose made up the clansmen of the southern uplands. The gathering of such a strong clan alliance was not to be ignored.

"They canna arrest all of us!" Robert Dalzell of Carnwath shouted in his deep voice. "A united front by the southern clans is to be feared and respected. The Dalzell motto is 'I dare,' and I dare the privy council to take on all the clans!"

After another hour of thoughts and opinions by the men gathered in the library, Sir John issued his judgment of the situation. He had listened carefully, thoroughly considering what feasible measures should be taken to free William from the tollbooth in Edinburgh, the fourteenth century medieval building near Saint Giles Cathedral serving as the main jail where, in addition to incarceration, was routinely imposed physical punishment and torture to those awaiting trial.

"Me fellow clansmen and neighbors," Sir John began in a deep, gravelly voice, his brogue more pronounced than usual, "let us wait for the king. Perhaps, God willing, I be able to persuade him to allow William to be released on lack of tangible evidence. Ye kin, I speak for me brother and feel he would want us to pursue this course. That is all for now, me friends, so let us do our best to enjoy the festivities our host has so generously provided."

The meeting of the clansmen was dismissed with the men acquiescing to Sir John's judgment of his brother's fate. Still alarmed over the arrest of their countryman, they muttered to themselves, shaking their heads and suggesting strategies to free William as they went their separate ways. However, they would await the king's ruling.

Some were unaware of William's involvement in warning the secret believers and his attempts to rescue those awaiting execution for heresy. However, some were concerned over William's covert activities, often turning a blind eye, for they would never betray a fellow clansman aiding the Reformation movement. Even the clans and households remaining loyal to the dictates of the Holy Mother Church, those ignorant of the New Testament doctrines, were weary of the burnings and sickened over the execution of the Reformers, their friends, and neighbors; but fear of repercussion kept many a mouth tightly shut in the Valley of the Clyde.

Peter remained in the library waiting to speak to Sir John privately.

"I cannot agree with your advice to wait for the king, hoping he will dismiss the charges," Peter said, facing his uncle. "You know that wicked cardinal, David Beaton, and the king himself, has searched for the Reformation Rider for years. And if he knew it was Father, the one he trusts with his mounts, he would be incensed enough to bring him to trial. Not only that, but father will also be held in the tollbooth. We should go in force, Uncle, break into the tollbooth and free him."

"Aye, lad, I'll tell ye what would happen," Sir John said in his authoritative voice. "If we failed, we Carmichaels would be outlawed, perhaps imprisoned, and our lands confiscated. Your father knew the cost of his activities—his mission, as he called it."

"It was his mission, Uncle, and he felt strongly that God called him to aid and spare the believers if possible. You never understood him, Uncle. With God as our Helper, we can defy the forces of evil and free my father."

"Defying the king and the privy council? Nay, Peter, we have a better chance appealing to the king and praying for a dismissal of the charges before he goes to trial."

"Is not Father's life worth more than being outlawed?" Peter's face was red with anger, and he felt hot tears of rage rising in his eyes. Already, Peter and his fellow Reformationists were meeting in secret, waiting for an opportunity to rise to take control of Saint Andrews and its powerful hierarchy that condemned men to death and imprisoned fellow believers.

"I understand your frustration, Peter, but what ye propose is far too risky. And ye kin, your father's life is worth more than all that we own, all that we have. That is not the question."

"Then, Uncle, what is the question? Why the delay?" Peter asked, his eyes flashing fire.

"Ye know, Peter, the Men of the Broken Spear do not gather the clan together in haste; neither do we rush to judgment. Your father is facing adversity because of what he felt was his duty; and adversity is a severe instructor, allowed by He Who guards our soul, a God Who knows us better than we know ourselves."

"You have persuaded the men of Lanarkshire to let your own brother and my father to languish in the tollbooth while we wait on God to free him?"

"Be careful, son. Do not find yourself on the wrong side of justice, or ye will learn obedience by what ye suffer. God can do more than we can imagine, so take courage and let God fight this battle. It is a fearful thing to fall into the hands of the living God, but it is more dreadful to fall into the hands of man."

Peter's hands fisted at his side, and his eyes blazed with anger. Never in his life had he shown disrespect for the Carmichael clan chief and his authority; but this time, he could not agree and could not contain his resentment.

"Perhaps you have grown old and fearful," Peter suggested, his agitation outweighing his caution. His voice trembled with emotion. "Aye, perhaps too weary to lead the clan, afraid for yourself, caring not what happens to your own brother. I cannot abide such weakness."

The intense blue eyes of Sir John Carmichael pierced through the brazen boldness of his nephew's caustic words; and Peter felt the unmistakable look, like a sharp-stinging sword piercing through his heart for his callous words. Sir John stared at his nephew, but he said nothing.

A searing pain gripped Peter's conscience, knowing he dared to speak to the Clan Chieftain with such blatant disrespect, but he felt desperate to aid his father. Without another word, he left the library and his uncle, slamming the door behind him with needless force, the sound echoing against the wood paneled walls.

Chapter 15

And be ye kind one to another, tenderhearted, forgiving one another,
even as God for Christ's sake hath forgiven you.

Ephesians 4:32

EXCEPT FOR THE SHARP SNAPPING of dry logs as fire ate into a vein of pitch, all was quiet in the library. Only Sir John remained in the oak-paneled room, his heart aching from Peter's brutal words. He sighed heavily; his characteristic good humor had vanished. He seated himself in an ornately carved fireplace chair with clawlike feet and a high back. His brow furrowed as he gazed intently into the flames.

Sir John tried to focus, to direct his thoughts away from Peter's assessment of his character, dismissing his outburst as youthful ignorance; but all the same, the words stung, tormenting his mind. Aye, he was growing old—that was true; but age was not a deciding factor in his decision. He had weighed the outcome of too hasty an action. Knowing the young king had a tender side, he would count on the king's sympathetic nature and trust God to listen to his appeal.

Cradling his head in his hands, his elbows on knees, he remembered that Peter often acted before he thought. He had a passionate nature, given to outbursts that cooled as quickly as they flamed. As a lad, hadn't Peter always been compliant? Now he was a grown man, capable, smart, and educated but lacking in the experience to rightly judge the minds of men, enemies that could not always be conquered with a sword.

Sir John was a soldier in many battles. In times past, when he was younger, he fought for the crown and then for Scotland, for the rights of his countrymen. He understood warfare, the conflicts, the struggles of right versus wrong, of nation against nation; and it seemed there was no end to man's desire to control and conquer. The tragedy of physical warfare was devastating; and at the end of the day, no one really won. He retired from warfare, from the conflicts and struggles, walking away from the endless battles. Returning to Carmichael, he sought peace that he found only in God and his personal relationship with Him.

Instead of dwelling on Peter's defiant actions, he mentally examined every possible scenario that William would face under the scrutiny of the privy council in Edinburgh. Except for the magistrates and royal guardsmen who had arrested him, not a single person accused him; and he was held prisoner on speculation and conjecture only. But he was guilty—guilty of rescuing the believers. And according to the Romish churchmen, this was a crime of treason punishable by death.

For years now, Sir John wrestled with his conscience and struggled with the right or wrong of William's covert mission. His brother was a man of action, a man of purpose who felt justified in his way of aiding the Reformers and the ongoing Reformation. But with the possibility that William might be caught and arrested, Sir John knew his brother would face the same gruesome death as those he tried to rescue.

Someday, somehow, William would not escape. Too many near captures in recent years were alarming and dangerous, sending a message to take heed to Sir John's warnings. William was the Man of the Broken Spear, disguised as a crofter or a royal guardsman on a Galloway pony, who eluded capture for years. The magistrates at Saint Andrew's had suspected him; but he was too savvy, too quick, and too powerful to be captured . . . until now.

Sir John had warned William many times over, even begged him to give up his dangerous mission and allow God to fight this spiritual battle, a warfare too big for literal weapons. But William insisted on forging ahead with his secret activities to save Scotland from the papal inquisition. And if William were found guilty—and indeed, he was—the house of Carmichael would be brought into question, and the entire clan would suffer.

The burden of his decision to wait for the king's ruling weighed heavily on Sir John's shoulders, and the responsibility of that decision would affect the clans and families of the southern uplands. And then there was Katherine, his sweet daughter who had borne the king a son, his own grandson, wee Johnny, a strong consideration for the king, a hope fanned by faith and trust in God.

For five long years, Katherine had been mistress of the king, summoned by him to remain at court for his pleasure. The king loved Katherine and was kind and loving to her; so she endured the shame, often persuading him to be merciful to the Christian believers held in prison. When the king was to marry, Sir John intervened, persuading the king to release his daughter from court to wed her one true love, Robbie Somerville.

With a weary sigh, Sir John knelt by the ornately carved chair, the fire warming the cold spaces and lighting the dim recesses of the wood-paneled library. He summoned faith, lifting his hands to the heavens, earnestly pleading for God's favor and imploring Him to use his early fond acquaintance with James V to spare his brother's life. He prayed that God would lift the spiritual darkness that warred against the light, but God whispered to his heart, "I will not lift this darkness; but I will send a candle, a trumpet, and a voice."

Knowing God had heard his prayer, Sir John rose from his knees. He would trust God to fight the battle ahead. When the young king arrived with his bride at Cowthally Castle for the hawking and hunting, Sir John would seek an audience with him early on before the royal guard had an opportunity to inform the king of William's arrest for heresy and treason. Even now, there was the possibility that the king would be met on the road to Carnwath by his spies and told of the arrest.

The interview would be complicated, for he could not lie to protect his brother. He would pray for wisdom and prevail upon the king's early acquaintance with the Carmichaels and his fondness for Katherine and his own son, wee Johnny. The king had confidence in William's ability to oversee the royal stables; and if William confessed to rescuing outlawed heretics, it would seem an act of duplicity to the king.

And for these reasons, Sir John hoped in the God of all hope, as he recalled the words of the epistle in Tyndale's New Testament: Now the God of hope fill you with all joy and peace in believing, that ye may abound in hope."[9]

Chapter 16

O death, where is thy sting? O grave, where is thy victory? The sting
of death is sin; and the strength of sin is the law. But thanks be to
God, which giveth us the victory through our Lord Jesus Christ.

1 Corinthians 15:55-57

PETER GATHERED HIS MEN, ZEALOTS like himself and eager to fight for independence from the tyrannical dictates of the Church of Rome. His father's arrest served only to strengthen his resolve to do something about the religious corruption in his beloved Scotland. But what could he do? Sir John had told him that resistance with force was not a good option and that prayer and patience would win the day. However, waiting had only given more power to the corrupt Church of Rome.

The advocates of the reformation met in secret to discuss the progress in the Highlands and Lowlands of Scotland. Many of the Highland clans dwelt in large tracts of land, removed from much of the ongoing conflicts and persecution of the Scottish people. For the most part, the remote clans of the Highlands followed the ancient religion of generations past and had little interest in changing.

But in the Valley of the Clyde, close to England, the struggle for religious freedom was ongoing. Several powerful men, influential nobles living near Saint Andrews, were involved in the religious system; but because of their sympathy with the Reformation movement, they maintained contact with those lowland zealots rising for independence from the Romish hierarchy.

In the dense wood west of the boundaries of Carmichael, woodlands now carpeted in springtime bluebells and narcissus blooms, the men, safely hidden in the thick undergrowth of the forest, met to discuss William's arrest and if their resistance group could do anything to hasten William's release. Some were Men of the Broken Spear, clansmen who were eager to aid the Reformers and help guard the covert meetings of the enlightened believers. Others were local clansmen, families weary of the never-ending occupation of magistrates sent to spy on them. Something must be done.

"Do ye have any news of your father's whereabouts in Edinburgh or Saint Andrews?" Alistair Eliot asked, running his long, slender fingers through his flaxen hair. He was a tall youth, long and gangly, who left his reiver family to join the Resistance movement in the southern uplands.

"Nay, no more than what was told to the men who were present at the arrest," Peter answered. "They said he would be held at the tollbooth in Edinburgh—ye know, the place near Saint Giles'. I understand that the place is despicable, overrun with rats and vermin."

"Och, aye, so I be told," agreed Hamish Cockborne. "And they torment the prisoners who refuse to cooperate, and I be thinkin' your da' will not be talking." Hamish stretched his long frame in the tall grass and rested his head on one elbow. He was eighteen years old with a strongly built body, curly red hair, and honest, open features. He was the oldest son, heir to the Cockborne Estates.

"I spoke with Sir John, our clan chief," Peter offered. "Och, ye know my uncle, and he is not ready to gather our men until he speaks with the king." A look of disgust crossed his handsome features.

"He, Jamie the king," he said grinning and remembering the times when the king was a young lad riding his pony to Carmichael, "is coming to Cowthally Castle in two days with his French bride to hunt." He shook his head and then said, "I am not in favor of this plan to wait on the king, but there is nothing I can do."

"I say we gather weapons, battle axes, spears, pistols, and swords and hide them until we be ready to strike that wicked Cardinal Beaton at Saint Andrews," urged Ian Leslie, a feisty, energetic young man, a zealot ready for action. He was a second cousin to Norman Leslie, an undercover Reformer.

"Och, Ian," Peter said, a note of caution in his tone, "it's not time yet. Aye, we are already gathering weapons and hiding them in that deserted stone barn on the northern border of Carmichael. We must wait, plan, and gather more information from our contacts before we ever attempt to storm Saint Andrews. Ye kin, it is well-fortified and will be no easy task."

"Ye are right, Peter," Hamish agreed. "I have word from our contacts in the north that the two Glasgow burnings did not set well with the nobles who are sympathetic with the Reformation movement. When everything is in place, I feel they will aide us in our efforts."

"Did ye know those men," asked Alistair Eliot. "Those men who died at Glasgow? Was your da' at the execution?"

"Didn't know them personally," Peter said. "But Da' was at the execution, hoping to rescue them. He was watched, though, and couldn't help them. Ye kin, I never go; nay, brings back me night terrors . . . "

The circle of young men nodded, some looking away, understanding the recurring pain when Peter, at age fourteen, was forced to watch Patrick Hamilton die in a slow-burning martyr's fire. Peter, along with another stable lad, had served as groom to the vibrant young Reformer, who was deceived into sharing his faith with the Romish clergy, who laid a trap for him. They told him they desired to be enlightened; but after his confession of faith in the gospel of Tyndale's New Testament, they then accused him of heresy and treason.

A man of noble birth, Patrick Hamilton was condemned to death; and his two young grooms were made to watch the gruesome death. The burning left Peter with recurring nightmares and a desire to embrace the Reformation to do what he could to honor Patrick's death.

Peter and the other groom, a lad of sixteen, were presented with a paper to sign, stating that their master had embraced the teachings of the English New Testament. They signed, unaware that their signatures would be used, along with Patrick's own confession of faith, to condemn the young Reformer to a fiery stake. Although innocent of the deception, Peter was heartsick. Remorse and guilt dogged his life; self-condemnation drove him to action.

"My da' was at the execution, too," said Hamish, "and he said both men died honorably with courage, praising God as they knelt at the stake." Hamish sat in the grass, his knees bent and his long arms encircling them.

"Do ye know any details?" Ian queried. "People seem fearful and don't want to talk about it." The young men half-hidden in the tall grass nodded, their eyes searching the woodland, always aware that an enemy might be lurking in the shadows. They were eager to learn the details of the latest burnings in Glasgow.

"Och," Hamish said, shaking his head, his red curls bobbing. "According to my da', it seems the two men were apprehended on a suspicion of heresy, having in their possession several copies of the outlawed New Testament, ye kin, Tyndale's version in English. They were on foot, coming from a secret meeting, when the magistrates mounted their ponies and arrested them. There was no way to escape."

Gordy Baird, a stalwart young man from Glasgow, always quiet and unassuming, spoke up. "Aye, and that be so; and it was no trial at all, just a quick hearing and condemnation, the stake the next day, burning the Testaments with them. Our neighbor witnessed the burning and me own da' told me of their heroic words and their deaths."

"What be their words, Gordy?" Hamish queried. Peter was quiet, not wanting to hear their last words but, at the same time, needing to know that the two men held fast to faith until the end.

Gordy sighed, removed a long stem of grass from his mouth, and listened thoughtfully to the men. He wondered if he should share what happened to the two men martyred for their faith. He didn't want to cause Peter a bout of night terrors; but if Peter were going to lead a rising of the young men who were also secret believers, he would need to understand fully the details of what he was fighting for.

"Ye kin the five Reformers burnt on Castle Hill in Edinburgh not long ago?" Gordy began. "It seems Cardinal Beaton was eager to make an example of any who defied his authority in Glasgow." Gordy sat up straight, meeting the gazes of the men who were listening intently with their eyes fixed on him.

"Och, the two men, Jerome Russel and Alexander Kennedy," Gordy continued as the group waited eagerly, "aye, they were examined by the privy council. Cardinal Beaton was keen to find other victims."

"Aye," Hamish interjected, "he wants to make a public example of any who dares to expose the corruption in the Romish Church hierarchy. That be his goal in all the burnings." The men nodded agreement, for they knew his words to be true.

"The men were found guilty of treason and heresy and condemned to death," Gordy said, "but Gavin Dunbar, Archbishop of Glasgow, disputed the ruling, wishing to release the men who presented a strong case for the gospel that inspired him greatly."

"I kin where this is going," Alistair said. "Gavin Dunbar couldn't take the pressure. He caved under the ruling or, should I say, bullying of the council."

"Aye, that be so," said Gordy with a sigh. "Jerome Russell, a young Franciscan friar, vera intellectual and learned, and Alexander Kennedy, an eighteen-year-old poet—both men outspoken—denied the use of indulgences, praying to the virgin for redemption, and the existence of purgatory. They both were condemned for heresy by the church council, who said they would go straight to Hell. Both men just praised God at this pronouncement."

Silence fell over the group in the wood. They knew they were not exempt from the same if discovered plotting and scheming against the Romish hierarchy who burned believers. They glanced around the wood, their swords at the ready, to assure themselves that no spies lurked about, ready to arrest the men of this covert meeting.

"At first," Gordy continued, "Kennedy near fainted at the ruling of the death sentence; but the bold, young friar, Jerome Russel, spoke to him, encouraging him to hold fast to the end. Then Kennedy was encouraged and fell to his knees before his accusers, there in front of the council and said, 'Jesus Christ is me only Lord and Savior, not the

Virgin Mary; and now I defy death. Do what ye please wi' me! I praise my God, my Lord and Savior. I am ready!'"

"God be praised," Hamish said, and the band of conspirators nodded, talking quietly among themselves. They were amazed at the convicted heretic's boldness.

"What happened next?" Hamish queried.

"The trial of Russel was immediately after, condemning him as a heretic, pronouncing the death sentence. Da' wrote his words to share his last testimony with others who might face the same end."

Gordy fell silent, as though trying to recall the last words of the condemned friar. Not certain, he removed a piece of crumpled velum from his jerkin and said, "This be his words, as told to me, albeit perhaps not in the exact order. The godless tyrants railed on him and spat on his person, but he was bold. He said, *'This is your hour, and the power of darkness.*[10] Ye sit as judges; and we stand wrongfully accused and condemned. But the day shall come when our innocence shall appear, and ye shall see your own blindness to your everlasting confusion. Go forward and fulfil the measure of your iniquity!'

"Then," continued Gordy, "they took them to the execution site next to the cathedral so all could see. The men were bound, tied to the stake. Russel said to Kennedy, his fellow sufferer, and this be his words." Gordy read from the scrap of velum. "'Fear not! He who is in us is greater *than he that is in the world.*[11] The pain we will suffer will soon pass. But our rejoicing and consolation will never end; we enter Paradise by the same narrow road that Jesus walked before us. Death has no power over us. Death was defeated by Him for Whom we now suffer.'"

---

10   Luke 22:53
11   1 John 4:4

Slowly, Gordy folded the velum, placed it into his jerkin pocket, and looked around at the young zealots who were determined to stand for the truth of the gospel William Tyndale had translated into English. Tyndale was convinced that the Bible alone determined the practices and doctrines of the Church, that all people should be able to read the Bible in their own language.

"Just three years ago," said Peter, addressing the group of men hidden in the thick woodland, men of the Scottish resistance, "Tyndale was arrested after years of hiding, fleeing from the magistrates, weakened by affliction, hungry and worn, then betrayed, dying a martyr's death. Let us remember these words and have no fear of death." He held a small, ragged Testament and read from the letter to the Corinthians: "'O death, where is thy sting? O grave, where is thy victory? The sting of death is sin, and the strength of sin is the law. But thanks be to God, which giveth us the victory through our Lord Jesus Christ.'"[12]

---

12   1 Corinthians 15:55-57

Chapter 17

And ye shall know the truth and the truth shall make you free.

John 8:32

AFTER THE RED HOSE RACE and William Carmichael's arrest for heresy, Peter rode directly to Cowthally Castle to meet with Sir John and the men of the Clyde Valley. Genevieve Chancellor returned to Shieldhill Castle with her father, who insisted they leave the village at once. It might be some time before Peter returned with news of his father's hearing, and Edward Chancellor did not want his daughter connected with this latest development.

Peter wanted to apprise Jenny of his decision to gather the Resistance leaders of the Clyde Valley, the young men of the Scottish struggle for Reformation. The men discussed possible plans to free Peter's father from the tollbooth in Edinburgh. It was risky business, and Peter felt Jenny should know the latest developments. With all that was happening at present, who could say when he would see her again?

Riding his pony toward Quothquan, the small hamlet northwest of Biggar where Shieldhill Castle stood on a gentle slope, Peter remembered Edward Chancellor's continued refusal to grant his blessing for them to marry. They were of age and could have married without his permission, but Jenny refused to be the cause of a further rift in her family. So the young couple simply waited. Jenny was convinced that someday, God would make a way for them to wed; but Peter was running out of patience. He had waited long enough and was weary of the delay. Once again, he would broach the subject of marriage to Genevieve.

Spring was in the air at Shieldhill Castle, a smaller keep that was the ancestral home of the Chancellor family, who had emigrated to Scotland from France during the Norman conquest. The morning mist lifted; and a sun-warmed breeze blew softly, feeling like ribbons of silk blowing Jenny's hair from her lace cap. She crouched near the edge of the pond, throwing handfuls of grain to the ducks and geese. Diving beneath the watery surface to find the grain, they created whirlpools of glistening rings on the smooth surface of the water while enthusiastically squawking and honking.

Hoofbeats pounded sharply along the wagon road, rapidly approaching the dooryard. A dusty cloud from the mount's hammering hoofs drifted on the morning breeze. Rising from the edge of the pond situated a little distance from the castle keep, Jenny shaded her eyes with one hand to see who might be coming down the road in such a hurry.

A young groom came running from the stable, ready to assist the unexpected rider. Jenny smiled. The rider was Peter, approaching the keep in haste. Seeing Jenny, just a short distance away, he waved a greeting, then dismounted, throwing the reins to the stable lad, who took his mount to be watered and rubbed down.

A young groom came running from the stable, ready to assist the unexpected rider. Jenny smiled. The rider was Peter approaching the keep in haste. Seeing Jenny just a short distance away, he waved a greeting, then dismounted and threw the reins to the stable lad who took his mount to be watered and rubbed down.

Peter sat down on the grass and pulled Jenny down beside him. He took the bag of grain from her hand, kissed the top of her fingers, and smiled broadly. "You look lovely this morning, my love; and I wanted to spend an hour or so with you, wanting you to know my plans."

"Your plans? But first, Peter, tell me about the meeting at Cowthally Castle with the head men of the Clyde Valley. Was anything resolved? Was there a decision to negotiate with the privy council for your father's release from the tollbooth?"

Frowning, Peter plucked a stem of long grass from where he sat, chewing it thoughtfully. "The meeting was dominated by Sir John, my own uncle, and the majority of the men present pretty much agreed with him to wait until the hearing of my father's case. But who knows how long that will take."

"Perhaps it will move forward quickly if they have no hard evidence," Jenny suggested.

"But, Jenny, our friends and neighbors in the valley have no dog in this fight, so they can go to their homes and wait until the hearing. I feel desperate to act, to do something to release my father from that despicable tollbooth."

"Your uncle John is never desperate to act if he feels God wants him to wait. He is a wise man, Peter, and it would be best to take his counsel."

Peter sighed, opened the grain bag, and began throwing seeds and grain into the water. The geese responded with a cacophony of noisy quacks.

"I'm afraid it didn't go well with Sir John and me," said Peter, taking a deep breath. "Ye kin, I was storming mad and disrespectful, unbelievably rude; and then I walked out on him, slamming the door as I left. I cannot believe I acted so abominably. Not a good ending, Jenny. Aye, now I am regretting my hasty words and actions."

"Oh, Peter! That does not sound like you. You were probably just upset and frightened for your father," Jenny soothed. "I am sure Sir John will take that into consideration. He is a kind and caring man, Peter, and he wants what is best for all concerned. After all, William is his brother; and he would not want him to come to harm."

"He might be a kind and caring man, but he is also an old soldier. Sir John is too harsh and set with his opinions. It seems to me that my suggestions are not worth his consideration. He is not easily moved away from what *he* believes is the right course. Even so, I should not have spoken to him so rudely."

"Aye, he is a strong man, but that is a good thing. Sir John gave me wise counsel when he sent me home after Papa beat me so unmercifully for hiding that New Testament. He told me to submit myself to Papa and pray for wisdom, to be kind to him and win his heart. That is just what I did. I admit that was such a hard thing for me to accept, to go back to my stubborn and callous father; but Peter, Sir John was right. After a time, Papa softened; and I won his heart."

"That was different, Jenny. We are talking life or death and not just any death—a cruel and brutal death by the bloody and wicked hands of supposed churchmen. For years now, Da' has warned the believers of impending raids on their gathering sites, of planning escapes for those found guilty of heresy; and now, he is facing prison or execution."

"I know this is hard, Peter, a terrible time for your family; but please, don't make things worse for your father. If you try to storm the tollbooth by force, you will not only endanger your father; but you will also be considered outlaws in your own native land. Then, who will speak for your father?"

"In all reality," said Peter, "all of us who are aware of my father's covert missions cannot speak for him without incriminating ourselves because we are aware of his activities to spare the believers. Only those who don't know the Reformation Rider can speak for him, and they can only vouch for his good name in the southern uplands."

"Then we must bring this matter concerning your father's mission before God, since we have no voice to defend your father and let God fight this battle," Jenny suggested. "This is too much for mortal man. The letter to the believers in the Ephesian letter says to 'be strong in the Lord, and in the power of his might,'[13] not in our own strength, Peter."

Peter smiled and raised her hand to his lips. "Ye are preaching to me, Jenny, my love, but aye, what you say is true, but we can be strong in the Lord as we fight for what is right. The Resistance is ready to take up arms regardless of the outcome. It is more criminal to stand by and watch the Roman clergy pronounce death sentences on fellow believers who just want to worship God in the truth of the New Testament gospel. Is that so hard to understand?"

"Nay, of course I understand the frustration, the urgency, the need to do something, but Peter, can ye not wait for your father's hearing?

---

13   Ephesians 6:10

There may be a chance that he will be freed. We can hope and trust that he will find favor. If you act before the hearing, there will be no chance for deliverance."

Peter rested his forearms on his knees and sighed heavily." If we can breach the tollbooth and rescue Father before an all-out alarm is raised, in the general confusion, we may get away with father and disguise our own identity."

"Och, Peter! The royal guard will be watching for you or anyone else who is related or sympathetic to the cause of Reformation, those who support its leaders and preachers. Think, Peter, you are already suspect simply because you are his son. I beg of you, wait for the hearing as Sir John advises."

Slowly, Peter rose to his feet and held out a hand to Jenny. His eyes were sad, weary with the strain of decisions too weighty for him, too crucial for mistakes, choices that could decide his father's fate and that of the young zealots who looked to him as a leader.

Jenny took Peter's offered hand and rose to her feet, brushing off her skirts and running a hand through her thick auburn hair. "Are you upset with me, too, Peter? I support you in every way; but I know that in our anxiety and concern, it is easy to make a misstep in God's plan. Please don't be angry simply because I concur with Sir John's opinion."

"I am not angry with you, Jenny. I am frustrated . . . angry with myself. I waver in my resolve to aid the Reformation. Do we fight? Do we wait? Do we stand idly by while the outspoken in the faith are burned and imprisoned? This is my dilemma, an impasse that makes me crazy."

As hot tears brimmed in Jenny's eyes, she gently squeezed his hand. "Let's not think of this anymore today, Peter."

"Aye, lassie, now that is good advice." He managed a small smile. "I want to speak to your father. Perhaps this time, he will grant his blessing on such a fine day. We can always hope, aye?"

The couple walked leisurely through the dooryard to the keep and quietly opened the ornately curved door. The Chancellor crest was carved onto a large, wooden shield hanging prominently over the tall entrance way. The servants informed the young people that Edward Chancellor had retired to the library after breaking his fast, and he could be found there.

Softly, Jenny turned the brass knob on the library door. She held a finger to her lips, cautioning Peter to be quiet. The oak door was almost always locked; but today, the latch opened, and Jenny and Peter slipped quietly into the room, hoping not to make a disturbance.

On hearing the slight noise of quiet footfalls, Edward Chancellor glanced up from his desk in obvious surprise, alarm registering on his countenance. In his hands, he held a battered Old Testament, His eyes widened, and his face drained of color. His mouth opened, but he said nothing. He seemed speechless, unable to say a word.

He stared at the young couple, his mouth opening and closing like a hooked fish. In his hand was Jenny's copy of the New Testament, opened for reading, the same Testament that was the cause of Jenny's beatings several years ago.

Chancellor had threatened to send his daughter to the parish priest to reprimand her; but Sir John Carmichael had intervened, warning Chancellor of the dire consequences of exposing Jenny's disobedience that would ignite an inquisition into her unlawful possession of a book condemned by the hierarchy of Rome.

"I meant to lock the door . . . always do . . . must have forgot," Chancellor finally said. He laid the ragged-looking Testament onto the smooth surface of the desk, a decanter of wine close by. With trembling fingers, he reached for a glass, poured the wine, and then drank a hefty portion, saying nothing.

"Papa," Jenny faltered, her face coloring in anger. "Have you forgotten? You forbade me to read or even have the Testament in my possession. You punished me severely for obtaining the wee book and sacked my governess. I thought you burned it long ago. At least, that is what you said you were going to do. And now, I see it in your own hands."

Silence hung in the open space across the desk, waiting for a response from Edward Chancellor. The young people had approached Jenny's father this fine spring morning to make another appeal for his blessing in their long-awaited marriage plans. On seeing the forbidden book in her father's hands, they had immediately forgotten about their request.

The shock of seeing the Testament, the unlawful possession of Jenny's forbidden copy of Tyndale's translation of the New Testament, in plain view and in the hands of Edward Chancellor demanded an explanation.

"Does this mean you are reading the gospel, a book forbidden and condemned by your own words?" asked Peter, his face a study of incredulity. How many times had Edward Chancellor accused him of being an insurrectionist, a follower of the New Testament, and using his own strong declaration of devotion to the Holy Mother Church as an excuse for withholding Jenny's hand in marriage?

Chancellor said nothing. He folded his hands, resting his elbows on his desk, bowing his head.

Tears welled in Jenny's eyes. She went to her father, kneeling beside him and trying to see his face now hidden in his hands. "Papa, Peter has asked you a question, and I am waiting for your answer. What does this mean? What are you thinking?"

Slowly, Chancellor raised his head. He was now gray with years. Glancing sideways at Peter, whose face was scowling with disbelief, and then to Jenny, the daughter he reared with such a heavy hand, he sighed heavily and picked up the Testament.

"Ye kin . . . Jenny. Ye remember . . . your own brother, a vowed young Benedictine monk serving the Holy Mother Church at that most holy monastery, Mont Saint Michel. What can I, his father, say? All that I did to gain him that coveted position in the abbey. What would he say to me?"

His face crumpled, small wrinkles furrowing his worn features. Years of unquestioned faith in a false system had betrayed him. Now, after reading the words of Jesus in English, Scriptures he could easily understand, words penned in the blood of martyrs and mocked by the Romish hierarchy he claimed to uphold, a book no larger than his hand had finally collapsed his lifelong trust in the papal system.

The sacred Order of Saint Benedict, an ancient order of vowed priests—men who made the solemn vows of obedience, poverty, celibacy, chastity, and charity—Edward Chancellor's son served as a monk in this order, a holy order sanctioned by the pope of Rome, the highest authority on earth.

Genevieve and Peter had discovered his duplicity, caught in the very act of reading the forbidden Testament. What could he say? He was guilty of that charge; but somehow, he must make an excuse.

"Ye kin," Chancellor said in a halting voice, "I be a devout follower of the dictates and traditions upheld by the Holy Mother Church of Rome; and out of curiosity, I thought to see what the fuss was about, so I read a wee bit of the book."

"You must have read quite a bit," Jenny said. "Your library door has been locked up tight for months, maybe years. Now I understand why the locked door."

"I never took you to the parish priest to confess, Jenny," Chancellor said, "so please remember that and grant me the same consideration. I am innocent of anything, except for reading the Testament. Not another soul is aware of this. I haven't forsaken my faith in the Holy Mother Church."

"Is that the truth?" questioned Peter. "How can you spend time reading the gospel of Jesus Christ and still be an unbeliever? Whenever men read the Scriptures, the Spirit of God will reveal error in false religious systems. I find it hard to believe that you still maintain faith in what is plainly false."

Sighing, Chancellor looked at both young people. "I will ask you and Genevieve to keep to yourselves what you have seen and heard today. Please, for all our sakes." By the pope and the laws of Scotland, Chancellor would be considered a heretic and an outlaw; and if he would not confess, his own conscience would condemn him. He had betrayed the Holy Mother Church of Rome by possessing and reading the Testament. He must never reveal to anyone what he had done.

Chapter 18

It is better to trust in the LORD than to put confidence in man.

Psalm 118: 8

THE YOUNG KING JAMES V of Scotland and his bride, Marie de Guise of France, arrived at Cowthally Castle with their entourage of servants and wagons of goods they felt essential for their journey. Lady Somerville had arranged the best of her guest rooms for the couple, and all were prepared for the days of the hunt. The young king often resorted to the southern uplands to hunt red deer in the grassy meadows and considered the fertile hills and wooded uplands of Scotland the perfect place for his trained birds of prey to hunt wild rabbits and squirrel in their natural habitat.

Sir Hugh greeted the royal guests with the deference shown to the king and his bride. Narie de Guise was regal, nearly six feet tall, slightly taller than her husband. She was raised in the French court of Francis I, where she was educated to wed a member of the French aristocracy someday; but Cardinal David Beaton had negotiated a match with James V, a Catholic king, which meant a profitable marriage for Scotland.

While servants cared for the grooming and feeding of the king's royal mounts, crates of hawks and falcons were taken to the falconry where Sir Hugh's own birds were housed. Among the staff at Cowthally, a skilled falconer was on site to maintain the health and welfare of the valuable birds of prey.

Sir Hugh accompanied the king to a handsome suite of rooms to make certain all was in readiness for the king's pleasure. After the king and his servants settled in for the two days of feasting and hunting, Sir Hugh prepared to leave the suite of rooms; but the king laid a gloved hand on Sir Hugh's arm, detaining him.

"Me friend," said the king, "stay for a moment. I have a matter of importance to speak of; and since you have made no reference to this matter, I will bring it to your attention now."

"A messenger sent by the royal guard arrived yesterday as we journeyed here, apprising me of the arrest of William Carmichael, my stable master at Linlithgow. From what the messenger said, he was arrested for treason. You are aware of this, aye? Is this true? He is my man of all things equestrian." The king scrutinized Sir Hugh's face, a stern expression hardening his features.

"Aye," answered Sir Hugh, meeting the somber eyes of the young king, "I was told of this after the Red Hose Race was over; and I must say, it is very disturbing, to say the least. After all, Your Majesty, William Carmichael is well-spoken of in all the southern uplands, an asset to our community, protecting the families living here from border thieves and ruffians and assisting Sir John in resolving various disputes in this region. I cannot believe he is guilty of actual treason."

"Perhaps not. But perhaps, it is so," said the king adjusting his jeweled jerkin. "The magistrates of the kingdom have been searching for this Reformation Rider, as they call him, for years now; and some seem to believe it is William Carmichael."

"What some may believe is not a certainty," said Sir Hugh. "Even his son, Peter, speaks on the king's behalf supporting the Wardens of the Scottish Marches."

"Aye, me kin, Peter is a valuable presence at the marches, working with the Wardens on Truce Day; but we are speaking of his father. Ye Carmichaels stick together like burs on a thistle."

Lord Somerville smiled.

"As do all of Scotland's clans," replied Sir Hugh with a knowing nod.

"Ye kin, me friend," said the king, "William Carmichael roams about the countryside . . . could easily betray me, his sovereign king, with little notice of those living in the border regions of Scotland. I trust William and am reluctant to believe he is a traitor to the kingdom, to me. Och, Sir Hugh, we shall see. I understand a hearing will be forthcoming."

"A hearing, a trial?" queried Sir Hugh. "Why not speak to Sir John Carmichael on this matter? He is in residence at Cowthally for several more days. His daughter, Katherine, is ready to go into confinement . . ."

Sir Hugh left off speaking, realizing that reminding the king of his former mistress could raise a sensitive issue. The king had released Katherine from her duties at court and made her free to marry Robbie Somerville, her only true love; and now, she was expecting their first child.

"I see," said the king, turning his face away to mask a hidden sorrow. Then he brightened.

"Aye, a good plan," said the king, "I bid ye arrange a meeting with Sir John sometime while I am still in residence at Cowthally. Sir John is a reasonable man." He sighed. "Known him since my youth. For his sake, I trust the arrest of William holds no evidence of unlawful activity."

"I suppose," Sir Hugh said with a measure of chagrin, "that depends on what the privy council—and the Crown, of course—considers unlawful activity."

"Exactly so," replied the king to the suggestive statement. "We shall discover the truth of the matter."

With a wide sweep of his arm, he continued. "After the hunt, the queen and I will travel north, making a pilgrimage to the Isle of May in the Forth. It is believed," he said, smiling somewhat hesitantly, "that a time of worship at the shrine of St Adrian can help a woman to conceive an heir for Scotland, of course; and we are hopeful. We will be absent from court for some time so arrange a private meeting with Sir John before we continue our northern progress."

"I shall arrange the meeting with Sir John," Sir Hugh agreed. "I feel certain that he can apprise ye of the circumstances of the arrest. He was present in the wood where the arrest took place and will know of William's activities, as ye say. After all, he is William's blood brother, the head man, and chief of Clan Carmichael."

Nodding, the king waved a hand to dismiss the subject. He was eager to hunt in the surrounding area northwest of Biggar, near to the village of Quothquan. During this late spring season, wild game roamed the lush green meadows where small animals were hunted by the birds of prey and the red deer came to graze on the tender grasses of the meadows.

On the evening of the second day of the hunt, Sir Hugh had arranged a personal meeting with Sir John in his own private study adjacent to the library. The king and Sir John met previously on cordial terms with other guests for the hunt and feasting in the great ballroom, where dinner was served to the guests.

Closing the door to Sir Hugh's private study, an office where Sir Hugh's personal records, reports, and account books were maintained by the Somerville estate manager, the king and Sir John seated themselves in identical chairs facing each other before a small fire. The study was a small room, perfect for private meetings.

"Ye wish to speak with me concerning William's arrest, aye?" queried Sir John opening the conversation.

Sir John had known the king since he was a lad when he visited Carmichael to hunt and fish with Peter. Before he was King James V, he had ridden the Carmichael estate with Katherine, Peter, and other youth of his own age. They had talked and laughed like all young people as they made plans for the next exciting adventure. Linlithgow Palace, where the king was born and spent his youth, was only a day's ride to Carmichael.

When Jamie, as he was known by his peers, became King James V of Scotland after the death of his father at the Battle of Flodden Field, regents, including his own mother, ruled the country. He was kidnapped by his stepfather, the Earl of Angus, who introduced the king presumptive to many disreputable pleasures; but Jamie had escaped at age fifteen and begun ruling as the rightful king of Scotland.

Things had changed with the trappings of royalty, especially after he issued a royal summons sending for Katherine as his mistress. He tried to maintain the authority of a king; but because of his youth and inexperience, that effort was not always easy. Jamie was now King James Stewart of Scotland; but even so, he felt the unmistakable sense of inadequacy and disapproval whenever he was in the presence of Sir John, this man of steel as he perceived him, like he was facing an opponent instead of an old friend.

"I was informed by the royal guard," began the king, "that your brother William, my well-regarded man of the royal mounts at the Linlithgow stables, was arrested on a charge of treason and that ye, Sir John, were present at the time of arrest. Can ye give me the particulars?"

"Aye," said Sir John. He placed his elbows on his knees and then clasped his hands, fingers intertwined. Looking into the eyes of the king, he said, "I was present at the Red Hose Race, where a large contingent of royal guard and magistrates seemed to have an unusual interest in our local foot race."

"The royal guard is present at all public events—magistrates as well," the king explained, his face hardening at Sir John's words.

"Och, aye," replied Sir John, his distaste for the presence of the guard apparent, "but they appeared to be focusing their interest on William. A person we trust, a member of the council, informed us some time ago that they suspected William; so I told him to leave the area. Seemed the magistrates were looking for someone to arrest. Ye kin, they arrest folks on a mere hint of suspicion, like a whiff of stink blowing in the breeze, aye?"

"I have asked you a question; and I expect an answer, not a conversation on your opinion. Ye did not tell me about the actual arrest, and that is what I want to know," demanded the king.

A flash of amusement crossed Sir John's features, but it was gone in a second. "There is naught to say, except that the royal guard surrounded William, disarmed him, and treated him abominably by beating him about the face. Then, they mounted him on his horse and took him away—stealthily, I might add—to avoid the crowd attending the Rid Hose Race."

"We have laws, Sir John; and if laws are broken, there will be arrests. There are laws forbidding any involvement with this so-called Reformation movement, laws that prevent the usurping of authority of the kingdom and of His Holiness, the pope, and his sacred decrees. Ye are aware of this."

Straightening in his chair, Sir John said, "Ye rule in Scotland as king; and if ye be king, ye have authority. I pray God will help you to remember that Scotland is your responsibility, not a foreign or political power that can dictate what happens in your own country, our own beloved Scotland."

"Ye seem to forget that the privy council in Scotland will decide what happens when arrests are made when laws are broken. If William has broken the law, the hearing before the privy council will decide his case."

"Do ye, king of Scots, not have the final say over the council?"

"In some instances, aye, but that is rare. I will not overrule the decision of the council if the ruling is in accordance with His Holiness."

"And ye, though sovereign, will not consider the right and wrong of a matter because the council or the pope of Rome has the authority to condemn or excuse a person? William is your own man, caring for your blooded horses, overseeing the welfare of the beast, and ensuring they are ready for the king's pleasure.

"And what is your point?

"Ye know him. He has been loyal to you as sovereign king and performed his work well. Would ye see him locked in that despicable tollbooth? Ye have the authority to release him. There is no hard evidence that he is the Reformation Rider. He has committed no crime."

"Answer me this, Sir John, and I will consider having him released before the hearing. Is William this 'Reformation Rider' who goes about the country warning the so-called 'believers" of an impending raid on their gathering and listening to the preaching from that outlawed book—I say outlawed, Sir John—that book written by Tyndale?"

"I do not follow me brother about the countryside, Sire. If ye do not have evidence that proves William is guilty of breaking the law and he is condemned, then beware, me young king, the entire southern upland of Scotland, its clans and people, will not stand idly by while innocent people burn for reading the gospel—the same gospel written in the pope's own Vulgate version."

The king rose from his chair, his youthful face reddening with anger. He was no longer able to maintain his frustration. "Do not threaten me with a clan uprising! Your words sound treasonous. Aye, granted, ye have power in the Valley of the Clyde. Ye kin, the border clans have always been rebellious to authority; but take heed, Sir John, ye may find yourself an enemy of His Holiness, who has authority to cast whom he will into prison."

"Cast into prison whom he will? I am an old soldier, a man who fought for this country, for justice, for what was right, doing no harm, only defending our country from the enemy. Never did I kill an enemy without cause. Ye are saying the pope has authority to disregard justice for any cause?"

"I am aware of your sympathies, your opposition to the burnings," said the king, his words dripping with sarcasm. "Katherine herself was so inclined and often persuaded me to release prisoners accused of sacrilege, and they were possibly guilty of reading or possessing that Testament. Och, aye, I know of your sympathies."

"And ye, me young friend," said Sir John rising to his feet in the presence of the sovereign, "have ye no pity for your own countrymen, for those condemned by the privy council, by the hierarchy of Rome, to burn a person alive for simply reading a book? Aye, then I am guilty of having compassion on humanity itself, on any who would suffer such a fate. Regardless of what religion they adhere to or what they might read, putting a person to death for reading any book is a crime against humanity."

"It is not just any book!" thundered the king, his anger rising. "That book has set on fire all of Scotland with its heretical work against the dictates of the Holy Mother Church."

"Have ye read it, then?" queried Sir John, his hands placed firmly on his hips. His formidable stature towered above the king.

"It is against the law to read or possess Tyndale's Testament, as ye well know, but you are avoiding the subject and refuse to deny William's involvement in this rebellion."

For a long moment, Sir John gazed at the king, remembering the young, fatherless lad, and his manner softened. Although it was against protocol to touch a king, Sir John placed one large hand on the shoulder of the king, and the king did not resist.

"Ye have sat at our table," Sir John began, "joined Peter in the hunt, borne a son with Katherine. Our ties bind us together, and I do not wish to sever those ties."

"Aye, but things have changed. I still consider William my skilled horseman, but this does not exempt the influential Carmichaels of the Clyde Valley from the law. If William has broken the law, he will pay, perhaps forfeit his life. I dare not be partial simply because of our former relationship or because of Katherine and wee Johnny."

"Let me say this, Sire. I do not expect ye to be partial, but I do expect justice and mercy. I expect compassion and understanding. I know ye to be better than to accept a fraudulent judgment from the privy council or from the pope, who has naught to do with this case."

"Ye Carmichaels, ye Men of the Broken Spear, are not easily ruled by a king, no matter the judgment. I am your king, Sir John, as well as your friend. Remember that."

"Aye, I remember well," acknowledged Sir John. "Let us pray that God will be the supreme Judge in this matter. The prophet Isaiah says, 'For the Lord is our judge, the Lord is our lawgiver, the Lord is our king; he will save us.'[14] Be a good king."

"Be a good king!" shouted James. "Aye, and what is a good king in your estimation, Sir John?"

Sir John said nothing, but his eyes held an answer too bold to say to the young sovereign.

"Say on then," urged the king. "I will not hold ye in contempt. I know what ye are thinking."

"Vera well. Did ye come from Linlithgow with your bride?"

"Nay, from Glamis Castle. I moved Marie into the castle on her arrival from France. It is far more accommodating than any of my other residences. And why do ye ask?"

"Because the blood remembers and cries out for justice, just as Abel's blood cried out from where he was murdered. Memories live in the bone and course through the veins. The blood remembers loves

14   Isaiah 33:22

and hates down through the ages, to the children's children and to their children."

"What are ye suggesting, Sir John?"

"Ye burned Lady Janet Douglas of Glamis just two years ago—confiscated her lands, her castle, all her assets—and then moved yourself and your bride into Glamis Castle. Ye burned her alive as a witch, although no positive proof was forthcoming; and then ye dare say trust the privy council? Will William find justice?

"Ye speak of remaining friends and yet dare speak to me of that witch?"

"I would say to ye, me young sovereign, with every royal decision ye sanction, do not let greed and power be a defining factor; or ye will surely live to regret it."

"Ye dare lecture me, your sovereign king?"

Sighing, Sir John looked at the young king with heartfelt concern and compassion. "Ye have no father; your stepfather kidnapped you, introduced ye to worldly pleasures that profited you nothing but illegitimate children and land grabs. I warn ye as a concerned father would. Be a good king; be a just and sympathetic ruler."

Chapter 19

May–September 1539

So that we may boldly say, The Lord is my helper,
and I will not fear what man shall do unto me.

Hebrews 13:6

DURING THE MID-SIXTEENTH CENTURY, EDINBURGH was often referred to as Auld Reekie, smelling and stinking of sights and odors unimaginable to the country folk of Scotland. It was a bustling town situated on the Firth of Forth, which enabled the inhabitants to travel by land or by sea.

The ancient walled city was crowded with run-down tenements, coal-blackened from cookfires and smoke. Putrid smells abounded, vapors of sweat, dung, and human and animal waste. Rats and vermin of all kinds occupied the streets, along with decaying corpses, putrid meat, the stench of spoiled fish, and rotten cabbage.

Alongside upper and middle-class elegance, poverty and congestion crowded the city. The affluent of Edinburgh lived away from the tenements in homes surrounded by walled gardens and high on the hills or just outside the town. However, business was conducted in the bustling downtown near the Mercat Cross and open markets where vendors peddled their goods.

Through the reeking odors of the tenements and streets clogged with every manner of refuge, the magistrates and royal guard escorted William Carmichael to the tollbooth near to Saint Giles Cathedral.

The royal guard pulled William roughly from his horse, kicking him soundly as they did so; but before they could restrain the agitated stallion, William managed to smack his horse on the rump and shouted to the confused horse, "Home, Shadow!"

The horse reared, its hoofs churning the air as he whinnied and snorted at being denied his master, and then pounded down the cobble streets southward. The mounted guard gave chase, but they were no match for the furious black stallion, whose only purpose was to go home at his master's command.

"Ye will meet with the privy council on the morrow," grunted the malevolent-looking man who had kicked him. "Need not expect special treatment here at the tollbooth either. Ye are just another prisoner awaiting execution." He laughed derisively and shoved William ahead of him to the tollbooth entrance.

"On what charges do ye hold me?" William asked.

"Treason and heresy, ye kin, crimes to His Majesty, the king, and to His Holiness, the pope of Rome, as ye have already been told. Now, shut your trap and save questions for the inquest." With this last statement, he opened a door that led down a spiral staircase to a narrow hallway. At the end of the hallway, he unlocked an iron door and shoved William into a room crowded with other prisoners.

All eyes fastened on William and gazed at him hoping he might have some food. Their emaciated bodies were filthy from long imprisonment in the tollbooth; some had open sores and stripes where they had been beaten. Squalor and filth filled every empty space so that some were barely able to move to find a clean place to sit or lie.

One small window was the only light in the cell; and from there, another stone building could be seen adjacent to their cramped quarters. One prisoner, a gaunt and shriveled man with indiscernible features, disheveled dark hair, and a beard, moved his ragged form a few inches to the right and beckoned to William with a bony finger.

Stepping across half-conscious bodies, William made his way to where the beckoning man offered him a space to sit on the reeking stone floor. William's leg was bleeding, and his ribs felt like they were broken from the vicious kicks of the royal guards.

"Aye, lad," said the man, "looks like ye might be a good catch for the Archbishop Beaton. This be the hold for prisoners who defy the king and the pope. I be thinking ye look expensive." The man looked at William's fine woolen tunic and matching breeches. William had been stripped of his cloak and clan badges that would identify him as a Man of the Broken Spear.

"Have ye been here long?" William asked the cellmate, who had offered him a few inches of space in the wretched room jammed with prisoners awaiting their fate. "I was told a hearing would be on the morrow."

"On the morrow? Nay, lad, they always say that. Truth be told, they get to you in their own sweet time, on the morrow or next week or next year—only God knows. I be here six months, according to my calculations." He pointed to some markings on the wall that served as a crude calendar.

"Well, why are ye here then?" William asked, looking around at his cellmates who appeared to have been imprisoned for a very long time.

"I be Richard Macpherson, Badenoch, and Strathspey region, north of Kingussie. According to the privy council, I be a political prisoner scheduled for hanging; but me kin and Clan Macpherson raised an uproar, offered that wicked cardinal a tract of land and some gold, which he readily accepted. Supposed to be released months ago, aye, but here I be, still in this miserable hole."

"I be William Carmichael of Clan Carmichael, from the southern uplands, Lanarkshire." William sighed, looking around for something that might serve as a bandage. "From what they are saying, I am held for treason and heresy."

"Och, aye, ye be brought up right away, then. They love trying heretics," Macpherson said shaking his head in dismay. "Terrible times, lad, terrible times." He spat on the wall next to the crude calendar. "Dinna think ye will escape the wrath of the cardinal."

Macpherson began to curse Cardinal Beaton and the privy council and all of Edinburgh, any who took away a man's freedom to rot away in the stinking tollbooth. Defiant and miserable, other prisoners took up the rant. Soon, they were overcome with weakness, and the curses died away.

William was not brought before the council for inquest on the morrow, nor on the next day. Not until three months had passed in unbelievably wretched conditions did the magistrates unlock the heavy door, and William was taken to stand before the council.

The council meeting was held inside a windowless room, preventing the public from observing the proceedings taking place during the inquest. The council members sat on one side of a long table. William stood before the group of men, his face toward them. Two disreputable looking witnesses, one a tradesman of salt fish and smelling of his trade, the other a man who hauled dead corpses and refuse from the city streets, both unknow to William, gave testimony against him, verifying that William Carmichael was indeed the Reformation Rider and deserved the death of a heretic.

The witnesses were then dismissed; and the head councilman turned to William, who stood unshackled before the bench. "What say ye to these charges, to the testimony of these two witnesses?" questioned the bored-looking councilman.

"I say the witnesses are false, bribed with money and land. I do not know them. As to the charges of treason and heresy, I be a patriot, loyal to Scotland, loyal to my faith, a devout follower of Jesus Christ. I have nothing more to say."

"And," thundered the head councilman on hearing William's response, "are ye the so-called Reformation Rider, grabbing condemned prisoners from the execution pyre? Are ye the man who warns people of an impending raid on their unlawful gatherings? If ye are the man, that is a capital offense worthy of death."

The head councilman was a pompous-looking man, his round, piggish face attesting to an appetite that consumed enough food to feed all the prisoners in the tollbooth.

William was weak in body from lack of food and the untreated wounds. He suffered further from the keepers of the tollbooth, who delighted in mistreating the prisoners; but even in his weakened condition, he possessed an aura of dignity, a nobility of character that set him apart from other men. He answered nothing, standing straight, shoulders back, his eyes gleaming with determination.

"Your silence, William Carmichael, condemns you," bellowed the councilman. "Do ye deny that His Holiness, the pope of Rome, has the power to remit sins and has the spiritual authority over Scotland and its people to adjudicate spiritual matters? Do ye accept Mary, the mother of God, as a divine confessor, a saint who is the queen of Heaven?"

William had known the risks and for many years was enabled by God to save the Christian believers from execution. He had one life, but he had saved many. Let them do as they would. He felt God's presence settle over him, gentle, encouraging, comforting. He was ready.

He took a deep breath, knowing that what he was about to say could sign his death warrant. "No man has the power to forgive sin," William began, "and no man can bestow forgiveness or take away salvation, except by the Lord Jesus Christ. Do ye not know the Scriptures? Do ye not know the gospel that clearly states in the Acts of the Apostles, 'Neither is there salvation in any other: for there is none other name under heaven given among men, whereby we must be saved'?"[15]

"Enough, enough!" shouted the councilman, who stood to his feet. His face red with indignation, he was in no mood for any challenge to his questions. "Do ye refuse to answer the questions?"

Weak and trembling from abuse, William remained silent.

---

15   Acts 4:12

"That is heresy, the same as in that unlawful Testament written by that heretic Tyndale. Do ye not know that he was captured, tortured, and burnt at the stake for his English translation, for denying that His Holiness, the pope, can forgive sins? Ye speak as one of those heretical Reformationists, so I am inclined to believe that ye are guilty of treason and heresy. The council will take a vote."

William was sent outside and tied to a post with strong hemp bindings. Wary of the crowd, of an insurrection that would free William, more guards than usual surrounded him. The crowd grew larger, murmuring among themselves as they waited to hear the verdict of the privy council.

Many lowland lords were present, dressed in their battle array, swords at the ready. Clan Carmichael held aloft their standard, the emblem of the Broken Spear flying in the wind. Their faces were serious, knowing that if a guilty verdict were found, William would face a death sentence. He had confessed to nothing, remaining silent during the questioning.

In a short time, the head councilman appeared alone, standing on the elevated platform where William was tied in his restraints.

"We, the privy council of Scotland, acting under the laws enacted by our sovereign King James V of Scotland and of His Holiness, the pope of Rome, the vicar of Christ on earth, do find the prisoner, William Carmichael of Lanarkshire, guilty of heresy and treason and to be burned at the stake tomorrow at first light at the town center. May God have mercy on his soul."

A roar rose from the crowd, whether in protest or acceptance of the verdict, it was hard to say. The uproar filled the space with wild clamor and jeers. The royal guard hurried William back to the tollbooth but not before he caught sight of Lorna seated on her dappled pony, forcing her way through the mass of distraught and confused people.

Raising her fist in defiance of the verdict and the sentence, Lorna prayed William would see her and take courage. William smiled and nodded to her before he was brutally shoved down to the cell in the tollbooth.

Chapter 20

September 1539

*I have set the Lord always before me: because he is at my right hand,
I shall not be moved.*

Psalm 16:8

DAWN CREPT OVER THE ANCIENT city, bathing the stone buildings and cobbled streets in a fine mist that, over time, turned the northern side of the structures green with moss. A gray mist rose and fell as it followed the changing winds that swept in from the estuaries around the Firth of Forth.

William was awake, waiting for the magistrates to come for him. It was the morning of his execution. The privy council chose a place next to the Mercat Cross, where public executions could be seen by the people of the city. Facing High Street in the center of town, the Mercat Cross, the market cross marking the public square of the town of Edinburgh, stood next to Saint Giles' Cathedral.

All manner of markets, public announcements, ceremonies, and executions were held near the cross for public viewing. There would be those in opposition and those who came just to see a burning. For this execution, however, the square was filled by the first faint light of day.

William had prayed all night, wondering why his brother had not made an appearance at the inquest. He thought that perhaps Sir John would offer money for his release; but even if money were offered, rarely was a prisoner condemned for heresy ever freed.

His beloved son, Peter, was absent as well, although many of his clan and countrymen were present at the hearing and holding aloft the standard of the Broken Spear. No doubt, this would be the last time he would see that beloved family emblem.

Yesterday, when the verdict was read and the death sentence was announced, he caught sight of Lorna, her hand in the air, pressing her way forward, her dappled pony forcing its way through the crowd. Tears were streaming down Lorna's lovely face, her countenance determined and defiant in the morning sunlight. He knew at that moment that she loved him.

William thanked God for this last glimpse of the woman who had taught his cold heart to feel the warmth of love again, his brave Lorna. He wished with all his heart that he could give her the green bottle, the wee bottle for gathering tears. During his months of imprisonment, he had pondered his life. Aye, he was the Reformation Rider; but he remained silent, refusing to acknowledge his part in rescuing Christian believers condemned to death for their belief in the gospel of the New Testament and for denouncing the unbiblical dictates and the corrupt hierarchy of the Roman Church.

He was not sorry; rather, he was thankful for everyone he had help deliver from death and imprisonment and for his years of work to spread the gospel. Aye, it was true, he would pay with his life; but he knew that capture was always a possibility, and he felt grateful that he had survived this perilous journey thus far.

He desperately wanted to see Peter before he died, but perhaps witnessing his own father's execution would be too much for his son to bear. William did not want Peter to become bitter and revengeful. After all, Peter had watched in horror the burning of Patrick Hamilton, a death that still haunted his dreams.

If William felt guilt over anything, it was that he had encouraged a more militant approach to the Reformation. He had done his best, but it was not enough, never enough. Sir John was right; there must be a better way. Though he sought God's will, he could not see through the mist and tears that clouded his vision.

As light filtered through the small window, William began to pray, knowing the magistrates would soon come for him. His cellmate, MacPherson, was released two months ago, and he missed the man who had befriended him. He was a political prisoner, not a heretic; so money and lands were exchanged for his freedom.

William could hear the other prisoners waking, their eyes shifting away from him. They knew he would soon be taken. Some nodded feebly to express sympathy. Others offered no condolences. They hoped there would be more food if another prisoner left the cell.

Leaning against the stone wall, he rested his elbows on his bony knees. His lips moved, and tears silently slid down his face. He felt keen disappointment that Sir John had not tried to free him. Sir John was a powerful man, with hundreds at his side. But hadn't he repeatedly warned William that someday, someone would betray him, set a trap, and catch him?

"Father in Heaven," William began in a halting voice, whispering his words from a parched throat, "I bless Your holy name, a name above all others . . ." Words came slowly as his throat tightened. "Now . . . I be about to leave this world; but before I go, I want to thank Ye for every time Ye helped me rescue one of Your children, for they are precious to You.

"Jesus is the Good Shepherd, and His sheep hear his voice.[16] Long ago I heard it, too, when Ye opened me blinded eyes and I heard Ye calling my name." He dried his eyes on the ragged sleeve of his shirt. "Ye forgave my sins and brought me up out of a terrible pit."

Lifting his head, he looked up and remembered the story of Stephen, stoned to death. Before Stephen closed his eyes in death, he saw in the heavens a vision sent by God, and his heart was comforted. William raised his hands to Heaven and continued his prayer.

"I thank Ye for mercy, for love, for sustaining me throughout the years. I humbly beg Ye to watch over me family—my son, Peter; Sir John; Katherine and her family. Help them not to grieve over much. They knew my work for You and that all that were spared was done for love of Your people, Your precious children."

His breath was ragged, his throat parched from lack of water. "Help them find the way through this darkness. Ye sent the light, and we have followed through the mist and tears of uncertainty. Ye led us to this truth; and now, we freely give our life for the peace of knowing how much Ye loved us."

Other prisoners close by could hear his prayer and were silent, respectful. Some turned their head, listening and nodding weakly as if in agreement; for they knew that one day, their time would come.

---

16 John 10:27

"I pray that Ye remember Lorna. I know she loves me. She will hurt for me. Ye brought us together that long-ago day when her brother, Henry Forrest, gave his life—a martyr for this truth. Ye kin, I could not help him, though I tried."

William bowed his head and wept, sobs racking his mistreated body, now weak from mindless abuse. His leg was racked with pain where the keepers had continually abused it.

"There on the hill where she was hiding," William continued as he remembered the day they met, "in that tangle of bushes, we found each other in the horror of that dreadful day. We took comfort together, waiting to be discovered; but Ye spared us, Lord. Now, it is my turn.

"Aye, Lord, our hearts melted together, softened by Your sweet presence. Was then I knew in me own heart so broken because of Maggie. I knew then, me precious Lord, I could love again."

The sound of the doors being unlocked and the screech of hinges from the upper floor signaled the coming of the magistrates escorted by the royal guard. There would be no chance of escape.

Footfalls sounded on the stairs, and the heavy iron key was thrust into the lock. The door swung open; and two of the royal guard grabbed William roughly by the arms, hauled him to his feet, and then half-dragged him up the stairs to the upper level of the tollbooth. He was too weak to resist. Lack of food and water, plus his untreated and festering wounds, left him barely alive.

The royal guard partly carried him to the Mercat Cross near Saint Giles', where an elaborate execution pyre was erected on a platform built high enough so all could see. On top of the platform and beneath were the bundles of sticks, nicely dried for a hot burning.

For this specific execution, Archbishop David Beaton and his entourage of underlings had traveled from Saint Andrews to be present at the burning of the Reformation Rider. After all, his bribe money and spies had finally tracked him down. Beaton was elated. A self-satisfied smirk raised his thin lips above his pointed beard. His money was well-spent, and he could expect the pope to be pleased and raise his yearly stipend.

The pompous-looking bishop in charge of giving the signal for the fire to be lit was dressed in his ceremonial habit, a heavy gold cross on a golden chain around his neck. He was making the sign of the cross and speaking in Latin to all present.

Archbishop David Beaton acknowledged the presiding bishop with a nod and then took a seat on an ornately carved chair provided by the privy council. The royal guard surrounded the archbishop and his company with a wall of protection, swords at the ready. Heretic trials and executions could turn ugly, and the royal guard would be ready in case of an uprising.

The bishop's final duty for the condemned man was to implore him to confess to the charges of treason and heresy. In a great show of generosity and mercy, he would forgive the condemned man his sins; but the prisoner would not escape the death sentence. If he repented, he would be chastened and cleansed in purgatory for some designated years and then be taken to Heaven if enough masses were bought by his family to make him fit for Heaven.

The royal guard and the magistrates stood William before the bishop, holding him steady whenever he wavered from weakness.

Though weary in body, William held his head up, his eyes bright, and waited.

The charges of heresy and treason were read before the people by the head councilman, and the verdict of guilty was verified by the privy council. The presiding bishop began to speak.

"Do ye, William Carmichael of Carmichael, confess this day that the charges against ye are just and true? And do ye confess before almighty God and before your countrymen that ye are sorry and repent of your sins against country, against God and the Holy Mother Church, and against His Holiness, the pope, the vicar of Christ?"

William drew in a long breath; and with his head held high, he cried aloud, "Nay, I confess nothing to these charges."

"Do ye not wish to be saved from damnation?" bellowed the astonished bishop.

Finding a burst of strength, William answered, "I am saved from my sins; from damnation; from lying heathens, unorthodox priests, and the pope of Rome, who has deceived the nations with his trickeries."

"Do ye not fear God?" demanded the enraged bishop. His face was purple, livid with rage at the bold assessment of the hierarchy of Rome.

"Aye, I fear God," William said with boldness. "But know this: 'the Lord is on my side; I will not fear: what can man can do unto me . . . therefore shall I see my desire upon them that hate me.'"[17]

An unexpected cheer rose from the crowd gathered to watch William's execution. The inspiring words of William Carmichael drowned out the noisemakers of the opposition. Shouts of "free

---

17   Psalm 118:6-7

him, free him" rose from the crowd, raising their fists in support of William. The royal guard drew their swords and quickly surrounded Archbishop Beaton.

Suddenly, David Beaton, archbishop of Scotland, cardinal appointed by the pope himself, spiritual leader extraordinaire, was gripped with a cold chill that traveled up his spine, ending in a circle around his neck. A dark and mysterious sense of foreboding—a premonition of something so terrible, so frightening—shrouded his devious soul like a heavy, wet cloak. His hands grew clammy, wet with cold sweat. He must get a grip on his emotions. Shaking himself like a wet dog, he attempted to shake off the sinister feelings of dread.

What was the matter with him? After all, he was the safest man in Scotland, living behind castle walls and surrounded by guards, safe in the knowledge that he was untouchable, feared by the people, a ruler of men. What or who could possibly hurt him, a sacred man of the cloth?

"Today, William Carmichael of Carmichael," thundered the furious bishop in charge, "ye, an unrepentant sinner, shall meet the devil in Hell for your blasphemy." He roared loudly so all could hear. Waving his hand dismissively, he held forth his golden cross toward William as though to drive out the devil.

The royal guard, along with the court officials and the regular garrison stationed in Edinburgh, were quickly summoned, fearing an uprising from the mob gathered to witness the execution. The mounted guard pushed back the people, shouting and swinging their swords until the crowd fell back.

A sound like rolling thunder could be heard over the noise of the tumult; and the crowd, fearing what was to come, parted like the Red Sea. No doubt, it was the garrison summoned to control the crowd.

From Holyrood House, the rumbling noise increased on the Canongate. Mounted horsemen, riding at full gallop from the abbey adjacent to Holyrood House, appeared in the distance, racing along the rough track up the hill to the Mercat Cross.

The guard hurriedly dragged William onto the platform. Too weak to resist, William was tied to the post by the Mercat Cross, the executioner waiting for the signal to torch the bundles of sticks; but before he could set them alight, the horsemen arrived. Sir John Carmichael, riding Sebastian, his dappled gray war horse, led the charge; and he was followed closely by his clan and countrymen, all dressed in battle array and armed for combat. Peter thundered up the cobbles with William's horse, Shadow, ready to grab his father and mount him onto his horse.

Sir John's shouts begging for silence rose above the crowd. The people quieted, subdued by the authoritative voice of Carmichael's chieftain; they strained to hear his words. Nostrils flaring, mane flying loose, and ready for combat, Sebastian danced in circles before the Mercat Cross.

The officiating bishop gave the signal for the executioner, now uncertain of what to do, to move forward and set the torch to the sticks. Sir John's claymore was at the man's throat in an instant; and the frightened executioner, backing away in haste, dropped his flaming torch to the cobbles.

In a loud voice that carried across the town center, Sir John shouted, "The king of Scotland, James V, has issued a full pardon for William Carmichael, which I now carry from Holyrood House, where your king has recently returned from the Isle of May, where he visited the shrine of Saint Adrian. He received a message from God during his pilgrimage, a message to pardon William from all charges."

Sir John rode Sebastian toward the officiating bishop, who backed away in terror. Handing the parchment to the bishop, Sir John waited. Behind him were hundreds of mounted horsemen, all making certain the pardon by the king would be observed.

The judicial committee members of the privy council were quickly summoned. The frustrated bishop presiding over the execution handed the missive from the king to the lord judge of the court, the head man of the privy council. A consultation was hastily assembled to study the parchment sent by the king to those in charge of the execution.

Shocked and outraged over this unexpected proceeding, Beaton read the signed and sealed pardon, stamped with the official waxed seal of estate and the king of Scotland's flamboyant signature. The document of pardon was no mistake. The archbishop was more than angered at the king's daring—a king he considered a bairn in nappies. How dare he! The young king must have been influenced to overrule the findings of the council.

This was an insult and challenge to Archbishop Beaton's authority, to himself, a ruling cardinal of Rome, chosen by the pope to be an advisor, an honored cardinal, an archbishop of spiritual affairs for Scotland. True, the king could overrule the privy council, but to commute a death sentence was rarely sanctioned by the king if a charge of heresy was confirmed. A decision of such magnitude would surely anger the ruling pope of Rome.

Chapter 21

He will not suffer thy foot to be moved: he that keepeth thee will not slumber.

Psalm 121:3

PETER AND SIR JOHN, ALONG with a dozen stalwart clansmen, gently lifted William from the sticks resting on the platform. Wasted and exhausted from the brutal treatment, he was nearly unconscious. No one attempted to stop the clansmen from releasing William from the execution site, not with a royal pardon signed by the king. The pardon was in the hands of the privy council and the archbishop, who was now boiling with rage.

Sir John dismounted his fearsome-looking stallion, Sebastian, who pawed the earth as in agreement with his master. Sir John stepped forward to address the council. His figure alone, straight and unbending, caused the council members to shrink away from the smoldering look in his eyes. He was in his sixties; but his age only accented his menacing presence, his supreme authority. He was praying that the council and Archbishop Beaton would not oppose this bold move to release William into his custody. The king had signed the pardon; but the council could request a space of time to confirm the pardon, even though the signature appeared to be authentic.

"I am taking my brother home to Lanarkshire," Sir John said with unmistakable authority. "And who can say if he will live, so grievous be his wounds from the brutality done to his body, aye, even before his hearing, a despicable act of violence committed unlawfully." Sir John's eyes blazed with anger, and his body fairly shook with suppressed fury. "Only the grace of God keeps me from begging God to open the earth and swallow the whole lot of ye, so cruel and inhuman are ye all." He swept a long arm around to include the assembled council.

Sir John continued as silence fell over the entire assembly. "The king sent this pardon to ye this day, by his own royal messenger, whom ye all know, signed by his own hand. If ye would take issue to this pardon, say now."

Cardinal Beaton rose to his feet, his lean body trembling with obvious fury, his hawk-like eyes narrowing to slits and burning with disdain and contempt. He addressed Sir John like the underling he thought him to be, a simple country knight who had the audacity to challenge the archbishop of all Scotland.

"Ye kin, Sir John Carmichael, that I highly object to this day's proceedings and will confer with His Holiness, the pope of Rome, on this unusual commute of a death sentence to a full pardon. This is outrageous! Do ye hear me, Chief Carmichael? An unfortunate mistake by the young king, to be sure." He pointed a long, bony finger at the face of Sir John. It seemed everything about the irate cardinal was bony and exceptionally long. His body was long and tall; his arms were long and grasping. Even his face was long; and his nose was long, seeming to overhang his upper lip like a roof.

"This is not the last of this so-called absolution from our ill-advised king," shouted the archbishop. "The pope will have the final say, and ye will rue the day ye defied the archbishop of Scotland. I will see to it."

"Ye say the young king is ill-advised when he says God himself advised him on this matter?" queried Sir John. A titter of laughter spread through the crowd.

David Beaton's face turned scarlet. "No more of this heretical speech!" the archbishop thundered. "On the authority of this ordained priest of Rome, I command ye to be silent."

"Your authority is not the highest in the land, sir. God's Word says, 'Their feet run to evil and make haste to shed innocent blood.'[18] I say to ye this day, 'The wicked in his pride doth persecute the poor: let them be taken in the devices that they have imagined.'"[19]

"How dare ye to quote Scripture to me," stormed the archbishop.

Sir John was not daunted. "'The wicked through the pride of his countenance will not seek after God: God is not in all his thoughts.'"[20]

"That is all from you and your kind," bellowed the archbishop. "Go! Get out of my sight!"

How many years had the archbishop's men scoured the countryside in search of this heretic rider, who aided and abetted the cause of the Reformation in Scotland? The archbishop was so furious at the king's pardon of the alleged Reformation Rider that he bit his lip in anger, drawing blood and tasting the dregs of defeat. But he would not cease his relentless cause, his obsessive pursuit to see this man die as a treasonous heretic. He was certain that William Carmichael was guilty, and he would set up another trial and pursue him ruthlessly until he could rid the country of him.

---

18   Proverbs 1:16
19   Psalm 10:2
20   Psalm 10:4

Sir John made no reply to the cardinal's threats. His outrage and fury had stunned the council into silence, his fury so intense that no man dared to object to his statement. His eyes were like daggers, and his entire being was like unbendable steel. Behind him, hundreds of clansmen dressed for battle stood ready, the Broken Spear standard raised in defiance as they waited for a signal from their chief.

At the forefront of the mounted clansmen, Lorna waited, her dappled pony prancing on the cobbles. She had come to see William die, to offer a smile of encouragement and a prayer of comfort during his last hours of torment. God had answered her prayer; and if William lived, she would be there for him for the rest of their days.

Any thought of the privy council refusing to honor the pardon, now in their hands, was quickly dismissed for now. The men of the council were not sure what the Men of the Broken Spear would do if Sir John raised his hand, the signal for battle; and they did not want to find out. The reputation of the Carmichael clan chief and his years of fierce fighting that had won him knighthood preceded him. His men were ready, eager for a fight.

Standing before the council like a forbidding nemesis, Sir John turned on his heel and left the group of councilmen, all shaking their heads in confusion, murmuring among themselves and puzzling over this unusual absolution of a death sentence. The king of Scots had overruled their judgment, the verdict they knew was the decision of the archbishop. After all, they were the highest court in the land— except for the king himself.

Turning again to face the council, Sir John paused and said, "Bring me his sword and weapons, his cloak, and anything else he had on his person when ye arrested him. Do not say ye canna find them. Be quick about it."

In a short time, a bundle of William's clothing, including his cloak, was handed to Sir John. There was no possible way that William could ride Shadow for the journey home to Carmichael, for he could barely stand. A wagon was procured from a townsman to carry William with the least amount of jostling over the rough wagon roads.

Peter jumped nimbly into the wagon to ride with his father. The emaciated body, so unlike his father, brought Peter to tears. He gave him sips of cool water and eased his wounds with linen cloths soaked in Coira's special ointment. He seemed to be slipping away, unconscious, unresponsive; he was but a shadow of himself, so gaunt and pale. Hot anger rose from deep within Peter's breast, and he silently vowed to avenge this cruel treatment of his father, and of all believers, if it were the last thing he did.

Vengeance was wrong, Peter knew. The Scripture clearly said, "Vengeance is mine, I will repay!"[21] But the execution of innocent God-fearing Scots who dared to speak out against the ongoing corruption of the papal hierarchy or for simply reading the English New Testament was also wrong. And to Peter, it seemed God was slow on repaying the enemies of truth. He would gather his young followers and find a way to stop this Archbishop Beaton from this terrible witch hunt for believers.

---

21 Romans 12:19

Chapter 22

For thou art my hope, O Lord GOD: thou art my trust from my youth.

Psalm 71:5

NO MATTER HOW CAREFULLY THE clansmen drove the wagon, every bump in the road caused William to groan in pain. After a time, Sir John called for a halt near a small loch along the southward march. The horses needed water and rest, and William should have a respite from the continuous bouncing movement over the unwieldy wagon road.

Sir John dismounted Sebastian and climbed into the wagon, settling himself next to William. Nodding to Peter, his nephew returned his gesture and leaped from the wagon to give his uncle a moment of privacy with his brother.

Sir John studied the deplorable condition of his younger brother, his body so broken, barely alive, only just breathing. He slipped a muscled arm beneath William's shoulders, lifting him gently and cradling his head close to his heart. With his free hand, he brushed William's dark, wavy hair away from his brow, purple with old and new bruises. This brutal treatment of his brother was like daggers piercing his soul.

A fierce battle began to rage in Sir John's mind, a warfare so intense that acting on his impulse to avenge seemed justified. By just raising his hand, a signal for battle, the Men of the Broken Spear would have wiped out the council, sent the archbishop to the Hell he had vowed to send William, and would have sent a bloody message to the pope of Rome to cease and desist his cruel treatment of the Scottish people.

But he could not. He felt the calming presence of God, a gentle hand on his shoulder, letting him know that He understood his thoughts—his desire to right the wrong, to act, to take matters into his own strong hands.

"Oh, God," he prayed, "help me to resist taking vengeance, to trust You in these perilous times."

William's head rested lightly against Sir John's chest; and then, from somewhere deep within him, gut-wrenching sobs tore from Sir John's breast, wetting his brother's broken body with his tears, wishing with all his heart that it were he who suffered, not his beloved younger brother. He knew William's heart was to save and assist the believers and not for any other reason. William felt his role in the Reformation was given to him by God, so how could he fault him?

Sensing a slight movement in William's broken body, Sir John saw that his brother's eyes were open, questioning and intently watching as Sir John wept. In a hoarse whisper, William said, "Ye came for me."

"Aye, lad, I came for ye."

Then William's eyes closed. His question was answered.

Carmichael clansmen stood around quietly caring for the horses. They filled their water flasks and waited patiently for this deeply personal moment of sorrow to pass, not knowing how to comfort their beloved chief. They awkwardly hung back until the journey would resume.

Lorna waited, too, a little distance from the wagon. She silently mourned with Sir John as he wept unashamedly for his brother, for his courageous clan, and for the hierarchy of Rome's unjust treatment of the Christian believers.

Wiping his eyes on the sleeve of his jacket, Sir John motioned for Lorna to join him in the wagon as he remembered that this brave lass had once saved William's life. Hoping for an opportunity to comfort William in his last hours, she had journeyed with the clansmen from Linlithgow. She was an uncommon woman, a lass of unusual strength of character and fearless in her love for William. No one needed to tell Sir John that she cared for his brother. William had confessed his feelings for Lorna, a strong and compelling lady who had miraculously found her way into his cold heart as though God had orchestrated a plan, an opportunity for them to meet.

She knelt next to William, tears of compassion and hurt sliding down her cheeks. Sir John carefully unrolled William's cloak and lifted his sword and several weapons from the folds. Then he spread the cloak across his brother's broken body. A small green bottle tumbled from the cloak to the wagon floor, and Sir John lifted it from the coarse boards. He smiled slightly, his blue eyes crinkling in the corners.

Turning to Lorna, he said, "This be yours, lass." He paused as his own eyes welled up. He handed the bottle to Lorna, and she took it with a trembling hand. "William wanted ye to have it. He told me so. It is a bottle for collecting tears, like it says in the Scriptures."

"Aye, me lord," Lorna said turning the bottle over in her hand. "God keeps a record of our pain, our human hurt. Our tears are in His bottle like King David said in the Psalms." She touched Sir John's hand. "I be thanking William when he comes to himself, when he recovers, and aye, Sir John, be comforted. He will recover."

"Ye kin, William will reason why I did not come sooner to rescue him; but had I come earlier, that wicked archbishop would have amassed an army to kill him, even before his trial. I waited, hoping for a miracle; and God did not fail us. As we all prayed, God spoke to the king, and a pardon appeared at the last moment."

"Would ye have fought to save him if he had not been pardoned?" queried Lorna.

"I did not want to fight, nay. I have done enough fighting in me lifetime, but I believe I would have fought for William," affirmed Sir John. "Seeing his ravaged body makes me angry beyond reason; but, lass, God restrains me from acting, from turning me hand to war."

"There is always hope when we wait on God and trust Him," Lorna said, her eyes bright with joy, "hope that God will make a way."

"Aye, sweet lass, we always have hope, and we have faith—the inspiration and comfort for all mankind."

Chapter 23

A time to rend, and a time to sew; a time to keep silence, and a time to speak;
A time to love, and a time to hate; a time of war and a time of peace.

Ecclesiastes 3:7-8

OPENING THE DOOR SOFTLY, COIRA entered William's bedchamber on the upper level of Carmichael House. He lay quietly, swathed beneath a heavy wool blanket. Turning his head slightly, William's green eyes searched the room for the old housekeeper's familiar face.

She carried a wooden tray laden with a kettle of warm beef broth and a loaf of hot bread straight from the kitchen ovens. Placing the tray on the table near William's bed, she bent over the convalescent and placed a comforting hand on William's forehead.

"Och, laddie, ye kin, the fever is not so fierce today, not as it was. Nay, me lad, ye are going to live." She smiled broadly. "So brighten up and let me help ye to sit up a bit and take some of this hearty beef broth. Will put the life back in ye, aye laddie, it will."

In a hoarse voice, William asked, "Where is Sir John? Peter?" His eyes swept around the bedchamber. He frowned.

"Well, that be just what I be meaning to tell ye—Katherine has birthed a bonnie wee lad several months ago. Sir John and Peter have gone to Cowthally Castle to acquaint themselves with the wee laddie and to visit with Katherine and Robbie, ye kin."

"A babe? Several months ago? Just now going to see the wee bairn?"

Coira plumped up the feather pillows behind William's head and then sat in a chair next to the bed. She spooned some warm broth from the kettle into his mouth. "Aye, lad, they didn't want to leave ye when the fever was so high, and ye were not quite yourself."

"Katherine has a son," William mused in a quiet voice. "So happy for them. And . . . is all well with Katherine, her recovery from child bed?" He paused, trying to sort out his thoughts. "I remember now. She was expecting shortly after the Red Hose Race, but then . . . " He left off speaking, recalling his arrest and the months in the tollbooth.

"Dinna fash yourself over Katherine," Coira said reassuringly. "From what I hear from Sir John, she is up and about, paying little heed to the rules of confinement. She says to stay abed for another six weeks after the bairn is born is absurd, especially when you feel fine and there be no complications, ye kin? After all, she refused to be churched and blessed by the parish priest as is the custom of women."

"Aye," William said chuckling softly. "That is just like Katherine, to be sure."

He pushed the spoon away from the housekeeper's hand and held her gaze, a question in his eyes. "How long have I been home, in this bed, Coira?"

"Well, ye have been vera ill, laddie, and death was knocking at your door when Sir John brought ye back from Edinburgh. Do ye remember?"

"I remember some . . . "

"No matter. The king gave ye a pardon just before the magistrates lit the pyre. Then, when ye got back to Carmichael, we all did our best to nurse ye back to health, to snatch ye from the jaws of the devil, from that despicable tollbooth, aye, and from that wicked cardinal, Archbishop Beaton."

William's dark brows drew together in a frown, as though concentrating. "I remember . . . seeing Lorna . . . somewhere in the mist . . . someone handling me roughly, tying me to a post, a dreadful pain in me leg, me entire body. But, Coira, I could not feel sadness or grief . . . nothing, like me heart was dead, silent, and cold, like God had forsaken me. Everything is so, so mixed up, Coira. I am messed up in me mind, aye?"

"Nay, laddie, nay. Ye are nay messed up, simply recovering from a dreadful experience, from a high fever and a broken body. Illness and fever will take a toll on the mind and the body. But dinna fash yourself, sweet lad; healing of the mind and the emotions, aye, it will come, and ye will soon be your old self again. Rest, good food, and time will be the best medicine for now. And, laddie, God has not forsaken ye, nay. Ye are loved greatly by the Almighty."

"Ye are like a mother to me, Coira, always so, after me own mother passed away. I can never repay . . . ye kin. Ye were young then, young like Sir John, he a few years younger, a soldier, me brother. Now ye are old like Sir John." He sighed deeply.

His thoughts seemed so disjointed, so fragmented. He wondered if the punishing blows suffered in the tollbooth had taken his mind, unhinged his thinking. Taking a shallow breath, he continued his random thoughts.

"Ye came to help us—from Ireland and your people," William said looking away, seeing another time in the distant past. "Devoted your life to the clan, to Carmichael . . . caring for us," he continued. His brow wrinkled in a frown. "Maggie died, but Peter lived." William knew he was rambling; his thoughts were like a thread of broken feelings long past.

"But, Coira, I do not remember leaving the tollbooth. I remember praying all night, wondering if Sir John would come. Then, nothing." Pausing in his random thoughts, his eyes searched the old housekeeper's face, questioning. His voice was growing weaker, fading away.

Hot tears fell silently down Coira's cheeks while her body trembled at the tragedy of his words. "Hush, laddie. Dinna talk now," she said brokenly. "Ye need to rest and . . . "

"Ye would not lie to me, Coira?" William said, interrupting her words. "Ye say I will recover, and will I, Coira?"

"I would never lie to ye, laddie," Coira answered with a sob in her voice. "Ye are like me own bairn, like me own blood son; and aye, ye will recover, William."

His eyes held her gaze; and with a slight welling of tears, he said. "Are ye happy here, Coira?" He spoke as though she had recently arrived from Ireland.

"Och, why should ye bother your mind with such an idle thought, me lad? Yes, I be happy, vera happy. I feel blessed to be part of this family, this clan, and never did I regret one day of my life here at Carmichael. When I held your sweet mother in me arms so long ago now, when she passed, I promised her to love and care for ye and Sir John like ye were me own bairns."

She laid one trembling hand on William's flushed cheek. "I could never lie to ye, William, never. Now close your eyes and rest awhile. Sir John and Peter will be home soon, and they will want to speak with ye now that ye are one the way to recovery."

Smiling softly to herself, she adjusted the blankets and refilled the water flask on the table near the bed. William was already drifting away.

Coira sat in the overstuffed chair placed by William's bed. The staff at Carmichael had occupied that same chair during the long days of watching over William. Now, as William drifted off to sleep, Coira allowed the tears to come. Hot and salty, they ran down her cheeks in streams, washing her face in welcome relief. William would live; she felt certain of it. Her heart filled with gratitude, and she offered a fervent prayer of thanksgiving, begging God to use her words to encourage and bless William. She prayed that her prophetic words concerning William's recovery would indeed come to pass—and very soon.

"Dear heavenly Father," she said beginning her prayer quietly so as not to disturb William. Laying a wrinkled, work-worn hand on his stricken form, she felt his even breathing, the simple rise and fall of his chest, and it brought a glad sense of comfort.

"We remember," she said, continuing her prayer, "that with ye, Lord, nothing is impossible. There be no prayer Ye cannot answer, no promise Ye canna keep, and no problem in this world too hard for Ye to solve." The dear, old housekeeper wiped tears from her eyes with the hem of her apron.

"With the touch of Your mighty hand, Ye be able to restore what the enemy has stolen from our dear lad. Ye can quicken his broken body, make clear his troubled mind with all its torments." She paused in her prayer, remembering his random thoughts." Aye, Lord, the brutal treatment was too much for most men to bear and too much to live through. But Ye spared his life; and in sparing the lad, Ye must have a plan all worked out. And, Lord, we say amen to Your will, whatever it might be."

Chapter 24

The Lord is my rock, and my fortress, and my deliverer;
my God, my strength, in whom I will trust.

Psalm 18:2

STARING AT DEATH WAS NOTHING new for William Carmichael. It had become a way of life over the years he had devoted to the cause of the Reformation, of warning the Christian believers of an upcoming raid on their secret meetings. His daring attempts to save those condemned to death for heresy had taken a toll on is mind and body. After weeks of recuperation from the harrowing months in the tollbooth, he was left with an unusual fatigue that lingered long after the wounds to his body had healed. He felt useless, broken, and shattered in mind and body.

Always in the back of his mind was the possibility of being arrested again; and next time, there would be no rescue. The pardon granted by the king did not make him less vigilant. He had unseen enemies who wished him dead. He understood that although he had been acquitted, the archbishop's wrath would use every means to find a reason to see him back in the tollbooth.

William was in the stable grooming Shadow, a task he thoroughly enjoyed. The mindless task soothed his mind and suited his limited strength. Suddenly, hoofbeats sounded on the cobbles in the stable yard. When the rider approached, William reached for his dirk, ready for whatever or whomever came down the pike.

He could hear voices and recognized the deep, gravelly voice of his brother, Sir John Carmichael, chief of the clan and distinguished soldier. William slid his dirk into a leather sheath just as a stable lad came through the entrance door leading Sebastian, Sir John's magnificent war horse.

William breathed a sigh of relief. He nodded to the young lad, who passed by the oak-lined stall, where he was grooming Shadow. The lad waved a greeting in passing and then continued down the wide hall to a grooming station at the far end of the stable. Sebastian neighed loudly and stomped the stable floor in anticipation of a good rub down.

Why on earth did he pull his dirk at the ordinary happenings of the day? William wondered. Was his mind so racked with images of the abuse he suffered in the tollbooth that he would never regain his mental acuity?

Aye, it was true. The trauma and helplessness he had felt in that despicable pit had weakened his ability to discern properly. He could still see the whip and the leering faces of the guards who took a perverse pleasure in jabbing at his wounds and laughing as they handed him food crawling with vermin. He could still smell the awful stench of the disgusting odor of unwashed bodies and the human waste of his cellmates.

The door opened, and Sir John entered the stable carrying a saddle. Seeing William grooming his stallion, he paused and heaved his saddle over the wooden railing.

"Och, William, ye must be feeling much better, like being out this fine morning. The countryside is cold and crisp, perfect for a winter ride." Taking a deep breath, Sir John breathed in the friendly odors of sweet-smelling hay, the tangy scent of horse, and oakwood and aged leather.

"Aye, brother, and that's what ye are doing?" William queried in a wearisome voice. "Riding about Carmichael along the borders of our lands? Is all well with our clansmen, no trouble along our borders?"

"Aye," Sir John affirmed. He could hear the sadness in William's voice, and his heart ached for the tragic sound of it. For years, he had feared for William, warned him, and dreaded every time that he disguised himself and rode out on a mission to warn and save the believers. So much was at stake, but he could not persuade his brother to curtail his covert activities. When he was arrested and declared a heretic, Sir John knew he would never allow the sentence to be carried out. He would find a way to save William.

"Several of the clansmen," said Sir John, "including Peter, are keeping an eye on things until ye regain your strength and can ride again." He knew William's lack of strength to ride out as usual bothered his brother greatly. "All is well around Carmichael, William. Perhaps the treaty agreed on by the clans during the last Truce Day will hold this time, and South Lanarkshire can have some peace."

"Perhaps," William agreed, "but honestly John, have ye ever known the treaty signed on any Truce Day to last? For hundreds of years, the English and Scottish clans have fought over the Debatable Lands, and it all comes to the age-old disagreements between the crowns, the clans, and the Wardens of the March."

Shrugging his broad shoulders, Sir John nodded. "Things are less violent since the young king dispatched the head man of those truce-breaking Armstrongs. Besides, the reivers are not so active in the winter, ye kin, so not to worry."

William left the stall and walked a short distance down the passageway, then turned to Sir John and said, "See this limp in me leg, John? If this leg wound ever fully heals, I intend to resume me duties again, guarding our lands, protecting our family working with the king's mounts." Suddenly, his eyes grew bright with unshed tears. William's nerves were frayed, and he felt the weight of his infirmity.

"But I fear, John, this damaged leg will never completely heal, never be the same again." He sighed deeply. "Those wicked men at the prison, guards at the garrison, they aggravated the wound at every turn, jabbing it, kicking it, making certain it would never be the same, perhaps lose it, take it off, ye kin?"

Anger, hot and bitter, boiled up from somewhere inside him. His eyes met Sir John's in a desperate plea for assurance, for something to dismiss his doubts.

"William, brother and friend, do not allow the worst of evil men to take away the best part in you or break your heart and spirit. Ye gave yourself, soul, and body to the cause ye believed in, aye. Now, ye must put the consequences of that work in the past, live for the present. Your leg will heal, William. And if it does not? Where we cannot see God's hand, we can trust His heart. He wants what is best for you."

"So easy to say, John, but my heart's desire is to help the believers. I canna aid them with this broken body, and they need help. But I am not as quick nor as keen with me sword or the ability to escape capture. I feel useless, finished."

"Och, William, ye are far from finished. It is time for others to aid in the Reformation. Ye can still ride your stallion! That be what ye do best, a valuable work on our lands, an important task for Jamie—the king."

The two men left the warmth of the stable and strode leisurely out into the frosty morning, heavy with hoarfrost. The world looked magical with the trees glistening in the sunlight like thousands of diamonds. On such glorious mornings, it was hard to believe that there was anything amiss in the world.

In the distance, the sound of hoofbeats approached from the south, and Peter appeared riding his newly trained bay mare, Bella. He reined his horse to a sudden stop before his father and uncle, scattering dirt and gravel in the wake of Bella's hoofs. Dismounting, he greeted the two men standing in the winter sunshine with a grin. A stable lad came running, eager to assist the rider. Peter handed him the reins and shook his body like a wet dog.

"I need a warm fire and a hot drink," Peter said, rubbing his hands together, his teeth chattering.

"Then off we be to Carmichael house," said Sir John. "There is a roaring fire on the hearth, and I be certain Coira will make us a hot drink."

The three men walked the short distance to the imposing edifice of Carmichael house, entering through the central tower. William limped painfully, his damaged leg slowing his progress.

"Ah," Peter said holding his hands before the fire that danced and crackled on the stone hearth in the central hall. "Feels mighty good after the cold ride through the frozen meadows."

"Where have ye been riding this morning, son?" William asked as he took a seat at the long oak table. "I be hearing that you are storing arms on that abandoned barn on Carmichael lands. Is that so?"

Peter looked somewhat sheepish and nodded. Coira entered the hall, bringing with her mugs of hot spiced cider. Sitting around the table, the three warmed their hands on the hot mugs. The housekeeper left for the kitchen, shaking her head and murmuring under her breath something about how William should not be out in the cold.

"I hope you don't mind, Uncle," Peter addressed Sir John, "but the patriots and zealots for Reformation are gathering a force; and we mean to fight back if another senseless burning occurs."

"Ye and the young men ye are gathering are endangering Carmichael by storing weapons on our land," Sir John said. "I did not give permission for ye to use the barn for what would be considered treasonous activities." Frustration and annoyance were evident in his tone.

Peter felt the time had come to speak to his father and Sir John. He rose from the table and stood straight, his legs apart, his fists clenched. He would speak his heart. After all, he was a grown man, and he could make his own decisions. The patriots for Scotland's freedom and the zealots for truth could not be stopped by simply waiting for God to act. God used men, and he and his young men were ready to be used.

"All ye need to do is look at Father," began Peter addressing his uncle, "to see what those heretic hunting devils have done to God-fearing men. The time has come to act, to do something to stop the archbishop and his supporters from burning again. Are you so complacent that such cruelty does not matter?"

The two older men rose, their chairs scraping on the plank floor. They gazed at each other, both frustration and compassion written on their features. William opened his mouth to speak but thought better of it and remained silent. Peter was doing more than warning the believers and rescuing men condemned to death. Hadn't he, his father, unwittingly led him down this path? Was his own zeal reflected in Peter's desire for physical retaliation?

Sir John began pacing the floor, his eyes flashing fire. "Seeing what your da' has suffered has caused ye to make unwise decisions, Peter. If weapons are found hidden on Carmichael lands, ye will bring the magistrates down on our heads. There will be no saving your da' then or myself. I am the chief, the overseer. "

"The magistrates will not know the weapons are for warfare," Peter reasoned. "Besides, they are well hidden."

"An entire arsenal for hunting? They be not so well-hidden that we do not know about it. Aye, we have been informed, but I was hoping this was only a rumor," thundered Sir John. "Are ye so daft, Peter?"

Not wanting to defy his uncle, Peter did not answer but bit his lip.

"I am ordering ye to remove them from Carmichael and tell your young zealots that they should disband and wait on God to save Scotland and its people."

"Och, Uncle," Peter said, "like they did Father?"

"Your father knew the consequences of what he did, and ye can see the result before your eyes. He did what he thought he had to do but not with me blessing."

"As do I, Uncle."

The room was stiff with tension strong enough to cut with a knife. Sighing deeply, William said, "Aye, Peter, it is true. I felt I wanted to serve my country, serve me Lord by rescuing those at risk of being arrested. I can no longer ride, not until me body heals. Perhaps never. Is this God's way of retiring me from me work to let Him control what I can no longer do?"

Peter ignored his father's words and turned to his uncle. "Vera well, Uncle. I will remove the arms from Carmichael lands, but disband the young men determined to stop this mindless treatment of the Scottish people? Never, I say. Never!"

The two older men felt the impact of Peter's declaration. He would act. Rage and anger fueled his behavior, his pursuit of retaliation. They could do nothing to stop his youthful recklessness.

"I can tell you this, Peter," William said with conviction, "anger or resentment never drove my actions. Rather, it was compassion and pity for our people and mercy for their sufferings, not retaliation and vengeance."

"Someone must stop that blood-thirsty Archbishop Beaton, no matter the consequences; and with God helping us, we can rid Scotland of that wicked man. There are others who feel the same way, and I intend to be a part of this Resistance," Peter asserted with finality.

The room was thick with a chill that rivaled the icy morning outside. Peter turned to his uncle. "I would like to know one thing, Uncle, before I take my leave and return to my work. If Father were not pardoned by the king when they were ready to light the pyre, what would you have done? I want to know. Would you have let Da' burn, let him die for doing good?"

The fire burned and sparked on the stone hearth, warming the three Men of the Broken Spear. Silence more deafening than sound fell over the men like an invisible curtain. Eyes flashed; fists clenched; but no one spoke.

After staring into the flames for a long tense moment, Sir John finally spoke, piercing the silence with his gravelly voice. "I would have fought to save your da', Peter, but God prevented it and prevented further bloodshed. Hundreds of our clansmen were armed, ready to fight for your da' and free him from the fire; but God had another plan, a far better plan."

"Och, Uncle, and ye dare blame me for wanting to fight for a righteous cause?" His clear blue eyes mirrored keen disappointment. Despite his valiant effort to keep his emotions in check, hot, stinging tears surfaced, and he shook his head in frustration. Would they never understand? Weren't they Men of the Broken Spear, always ready for battle?

Peter faced down his father and uncle, who were standing silent before the warmth of the blazing fire. He loved these men most in the world, the men who had raised him, taught him the meaning of courage and valor and of faith in God and in himself, men who made him proud of who he was.

Disappointed in their lack of support, Peter abruptly turned away and walked out into the frosty winter morning, slamming the heavy oak door behind him, his boots echoing loudly on the wooden planking.

Chapter 25

December 1542

Solway Moss

This poor man cried, and the LORD heard him,
and saved him out of all his troubles.

Psalm 34:6

PRIOR TO 1542, KING HENRY VIII of England, James V's uncle, broke all loyalties with the pope and the Roman Catholic Church and declared himself to be head over the Church of England. He then began methodically to dissolve and destroy the monasteries and abbeys throughout the countryside.

He urged James to do the same and follow his lead for Reformation by breaking ties with the Holy Mother Church of Rome. James, a devout Catholic with a French Catholic wife and a hefty annual stipend from Rome, stubbornly refused.

After James continually insulted his uncle by refusing to abandon his faith in the pope and the Roman Church, Henry was beyond furious. He arranged a meeting with James at York, a significant city in the far north of England to further discuss concerns over the corruption of the Romish hierarchy; but James, not liking the territory and knowing his uncle's temper, did not show up. James' failure to appear angered King Henry so much that he gathered his army to invade Scotland and force the Scots to comply.

At the urging of King James, clans of the southern uplands of Scotland and enlisted Scottish soldiers joined forces to stop the invasion of English troops into Scottish territory. While many supported King Henry's break from Catholicism, they did not want England to invade their country to force a united alliance simply for religious reform.

James assembled his Scottish troops, and his army marched southeast to meet Henry's well experienced army. On November 24, 1542, Scotland was soundly defeated at the Battle of Solway Moss on the Scottish/English Border. James V himself was not at the battlefront and, after hearing of the terrible defeat, was so disheartened at the news that he immediately left for Falkland Palace.

Peter Carmichael of Carmichael lay wounded miles from the River Esk, where much of the fighting occurred. He had hidden in the bogs, escaping notice of the English soldiers who were hunting stragglers making their way through the marshy landscape. His injuries were not fatal. A sword slash across the ribs failed to penetrate the inner body, but loss of blood and lack of food and water had weakened him. He had slowly crawled west, sometimes ducking beneath the swampy waters as soldiers passed just feet away from his hiding place.

Now, he lay flat out on dry turf beneath some scrubby brush, hoping the English soldiers had not ventured this far across the border. He knew he must keep moving through this desolate and empty borderland until he could reach a crofter's cottage and beg for food and water, but he was too weak to move. He would probably die here, another nameless casualty of war.

As Peter's mind wandered in and out of consciousness, he recalled from depths of weariness his uncle's words spoken in his melodic brogue before he left for the battle. "To avoid war, speak calmly and wisely and keep an impressive arsenal close at hand. That be power without conflict."

The battle at Solway Moss was a knee-jerk reaction on King Henry's part when his request for unity was denied by James V of Scotland. Perhaps, Peter thought, his uncle was right. The Scots had no impressive army or arsenal, only clansmen hoping to win by brute force. Negotiations in York may have avoided the senseless loss of lives and the humiliation of the devastated and retreating Scots.

A leather boot kicking his wounded ribs brought Peter to wakefulness with a muffled groan. He opened his eyes to see a large man standing over him, his weather-worn face expressing a measure of amusement.

"Och, ye be awake, not dead yet," the man observed. The large, brawny giant knelt to get a better look at Peter, assessing his wounds and his wasted body.

Squinting narrowly at the man through dull eyes, Peter asked in a throaty voice, "Where am I?" He could see the swarthy-looking man was a Scot, not a soldier from Henry's army. He must be beyond the English army's search for stragglers. Several yards away, he saw a large Destrier war horse munching on some scrubby grass.

"Ye be a few miles from Larriston Tower," the stranger said in a deep voice. Then, he opened Peter's blood-soaked tunic to see the sword wound across his ribs. Peter attempted to rise but fell back on the turf, his naked wound still seeping blood.

"Ye are not dying of this wound," said the grizzled man with a wicked grin. "Aye, lad, perhaps from pure humiliation!" He laughed uproariously, as though Peter's appalling condition brought him some kind of perverse pleasure. The man strode casually to his war horse and untied a skin of water. Kneeling by Peter, he lifted Peter's head and held the refreshing water to his lips.

Peter drank the cool, clear water and immediately felt strength returning to his body. Earlier, in desperation, thirsty and weak, he had drunk from the bog, only to make himself sick from the slimy water. The pure water the man had offered him would surely sustain his life until he reached Carmichael lands.

Groaning, Peter said, "Larriston Tower."

He tried desperately to recall where Larriston Tower was located and which clan family claimed the territory. He may have escaped from the English soldiers, but now he was deep in enemy territory, that of the notorious border reivers. Many strong and imposing stone towers were situated along the Scottish/English border lands, protecting their clan territory from invaders pillaging for cattle and other goods.

"Are you an Elliot then?" Peter queried cautiously.

On occasion, Peter vaguely remembered the area. He had been present on Truce Day when border reivers negotiated with the Wardens of the March on both sides of the border. The treaty was an attempt to pursue a peace agreement that never held for long.

"Aye, I be an Elliot. Jock Elliot, head man of the Elliot clan; and ye be young Carmichael. Saw ye one Truce Day. Your da' be there, too."

He laughed again, as if Truce Day was a huge joke. "Your da' be always watching the borders of Carmichael lands. I see him on that black stallion, but he never sees me. I be a master at hiding meself."

Larriston Tower, Peter thought, his mind returning to the reiver clans who came together at Liddesdale on Truce Day. Och, aye, he knew of the Elliot family. Little Jock Elliot was a notorious outlaw, a Scottish reiver, an infamous plunderer and cattle-lifter, a thief from the powerful Elliot family living at Larriston Tower near the lawless Scottish border.

"What dares meddle with you," Peter translated weakly. "Dinna fash yourself, Elliot. I be in no condition to bother with your life, your family, or anyone else in the border lands. Just want to get home, that is all."

"Ye may want to get home; but ye will never make it, nay, not until ye rest, lad." Elliot whistled for his horse grazing nearby. The skies were threatening rain, and the wind was picking up.

Jock Elliot scanned the sky and put a finger in the wind. "Will take you to the tower before this storm hits. Rest there for a few days, eat some good food, drink some cool water, and tend those wounds, ye kin? Then, lad, ye be in decent shape to ask for a ransom." He bellowed a laugh and began to haul Peter from beneath the brush.

"Aye, is well I have me war horse wi' me today, not me pony. Ye can ride pillion wi' me to the tower not vera far from here." Elliot smiled roguishly before saying, "I have no grudge wi' Chief Carmichael—or agin' any Carmichaels, for that matter. The lands be too far north to escape wi' beasts in tow, though, I must admit, those fat beef cattle be vera tempting, indeed they do."

"I will be grateful if you can help me and take me to your tower house until I gain my strength. Then, I be on my way," Peter said weakly. He was not sure he could trust Little Jock, but he had no choice. He was too weak to go any further, and he would surely die if left here with no food or water and with his wounds left untended.

"Och," said Jock rubbing his bearded chin, "I be thinkin' the chief of Carmichael just might offer a few of those fat cattle to pay for your rescue from certain death and, of course, for the excellent care you will receive at Larriston Tower. Is that not so, young Carmichael?"

It was abundantly clear to Peter that a ransom would be required. Little Jock Elliot would hold him at the tower for ransom—in a nice way, of course, not wanting to threaten Clan Carmichael with an actual demand for payment but just an exchange of cattle for rescuing him. Peter sighed, knowing the border outlaw would take advantage of his weakened condition that just happened to be on Elliot lands—and do it with a smile on his rugged face.

On Peter's arrival at Larriston Tower, a message was sent to Sir John stating that his nephew was rescued by Clan Elliot and was receiving excellent care. He would be returned to Carmichael in good health, of course. No money would be necessary for the excellent care of the wounded Peter—just a few cattle to pay for expenses.

When the message arrived, Sir John understood perfectly. It was indeed a ransom; and he would pay with cattle, or Peter would remain a captive at Larriston Tower. This was Little Jock's advantageous style of stealing cattle instead of the usual raid.

The Elliot clan, outlaws and raiders, met with the Scottish Warden on Truce Day to propose a "cease and desist" of raiding on both sides of the border; but Jock Elliot gave little heed to the rules.

True to his word, the infamous border reiver and the Elliot family housed at the tower provided the best of care for Peter's weakened body. In a short time, Peter recovered enough to travel. He was escorted by fifty delighted Elliot clansmen to the southern borders of Carmichael lands. As they rode their Galloway ponies, they laughed and sang the old Scottish ballads so loved by the border outlaws. Little Jock himself led the band, his deep bass bellowing his delight over this easy conquest.

Twenty Carmichael clansmen, grim and silent, herded ten ready-for-market beef cattle to the waiting Elliot clansmen for the exchange. Little Jock Elliot led Peter's pony to the safety of the Carmichael men waiting, their swords at the ready. Little Jock laughed, tipping his hat and waving in good humor as his men rounded up the cattle and herded them away with whoops of laughter. Little Jock rode to where Sir John and William, eager for this exchange to be over, sat astride their mounts.

"As ye can see, Chief Carmichael, your nephew returns in good health"—Elliot paused, his eyes twinkling with mirth—"although he seems a wee bit low in spirits. The lad was treated well, aye, upon my word. I be thankin' ye, Chief Carmichael, for the fat cattle agreed upon for the care of the lad, aye?"

Sir John nodded. "We both understand the truth of this exchange, Elliot. I have kept me word and don't expect your men to shadow my lands again."

Lifting his hat and grinning broadly, Elliot nodded amicably to Sir John and waved a jaunty farewell to the Carmichael men who would have eagerly pursued the merry outlaws had Sir John given them leave. As the dust rose above the retreating Elliots, they could hear Little Jock's laughter and the wild cheering of his men echoing across the distant hills in the Valley of the Clyde.

"And a merry Yule tide to ye all," old Jock Elliot shouted with a laugh.

Peter mounted his pony, then spoke to his uncle. "Thank you, Uncle, for paying the outrageous ransom, "

"Aye, lad, if I were to use a standard of measurement for this exchange—beef cattle for a young, sometimes foolish lad—then I would underestimate the value of your life. The most important principle in life is not what you get but what you can give, what you can become. Old Jock gets me cattle, but I gladly paid the ransom for your life. Remember this, lad."

Chapter 26

But thou, O LORD, art a shield for me; my glory, and the lifter up of mine head.

Psalm 3:3

AT COWTHALLY CASTLE, KATHERINE AND Lady Somerville were weaving together long garlands of spruce, pine, and fir boughs and tying them off with loops of red satin ribbon. The woodsy fragrance filled the banqueting hall, where a huge log fire sparked and crackled on the flagstone hearth. A festive mood warmed the hall, ushering in the Advent season of early December, but the recent invasion of King Henry's army into Scotland's southern border overshadowed the cheerful atmosphere.

Even so, the entire month was given over to celebrating the birth of Christ. The twelve days of feasting and merry-making would begin on December 25 and last through January 5. The entire household of the Carmichael family was invited to join the Somervilles in celebrating the joyful season. A plump pig and young beef were slaughtered in November and smoked in preparation for the Yule tide dinner.

With boundless energy, the two little boys—wee Johnny, now eight years old, and Baby Robbie Somerville, just four years old—were excitedly running about the hall, whooping and laughing, playing around the huge pile of greenery.

"Will you boys please be careful," scolded Lady Somerville. "You could slip and fall on these treacherous pine needles. Then what will we do if you break a leg?"

The boys stopped running, looked at each other, then jumped into the huge pile of discarded branches, laughing with boyish delight.

A sudden loud knocking at the double doors of the end of the hall sent a servant hurrying to open the doors. A liveried messenger carrying a single letter was ushered into the hall. Lady Somerville motioned for the unexpected messenger to approach.

Bowing slightly and scattering pine needles in his wake, he said, "Pardon me, m'lady, a message from the king." Handing Katherine a velum letter with the king's seal stamped in wax, the messenger withdrew a few paces and waited silently while Katherine read the missive.

Seeing Katherine's face turn pale, Lady Somerville went to her side and beckoned for a servant to take the boys to the nursery. Katherine hesitated, saying nothing.

"What is it, Katherine?" asked Lady Somerville, slipping an arm around Katherine's waist. "Is there news of Peter? Has he been hurt, taken captive? Sorry, Katherine, I am just so anxious."

"Och, dear lady, there was fierce fighting at Solway Moss," Katherine said in a halting voice, "and the Scots were badly beaten, retreating from the battle and further conflict. The king fled to Falkland Palace and is asking that I join him there. He is ill and requests that I come immediately."

"M'lady," the servant said bowing slightly, "as requested by His Royal Highness, the king's own carriage and horses are awaiting in the bailey to bring you to Falkland."

"Is it that urgent?" Katherine asked, speaking to the messenger.

"Aye, m'lady, the king is extremely troubled and requests your presence at once. I canna say, but I believe he is close to the end."

"Oh, no! Was he wounded in battle?" Katherine asked, her distress obvious.

"Nay, not wounded in his body, m'lady, but his mind is . . . he is not himself and refuses to eat nor sleep. I beg of ye to gather your things and bring your husband and come at once . . . before it is too late."

"My husband and our men folk are hunting all day and aren't planning to be back until dusk," Katherine said, glancing at the king's message, her hands trembling nervously. Turning to Lady Somerville, she asked, "What should I do, dear lady?"

"Indeed, you must go, Katherine. If the king requests your presence, then you must not delay. I will send Robbie to Falkland when the men return from the hunt. Since the king is Johnny's father, no doubt he will have instructions for the lad. Go now; make haste, Katherine. It is extremely cold outside, so take your warmest cloak for the trip to Falkland. I will watch over the boys. They are perfectly comfortable here."

A short time later, Katherine, wrapped in her fur cloak, was seated aboard the impressively outfitted royal carriage traveling along the wagon road to Falkland Palace, just seventeen miles west of Linlithgow, where the king had gone for refuge from the disastrous battle at Solway Moss. Eight outriders accompanied the royal carriage, four stalwart guardsmen riding before the carriage and four bringing up the rear.

They journeyed northwest to the palatial estate, where King James V awaited Katherine's arrival. In winter, the extensive gardens surrounding the palace were dormant, and now the winding road leading to the gated entrance was covered with snow. The winter season was unusually cold this year, making traveling any distance quite difficult. As fast as the snow piled into drifts, the strong winds blew it away.

The walled gardens led to the formal entrance of the Renaissance palace. Ornately woven Flemish tapestries so loved by the young king decorated the banqueting hall, and the king had spared no expense to obtain the beautifully woven tapestries. Talented artisans crafted murals on the ceilings with detailed paintings purposely created to impress visitors to the royal palace.

On her arrival, Katherine was immediately escorted by the king's most trusted servants to his bed chamber, where King James V lay on his bed surrounded by physicians, lawyers, and advisors of the royal court, who appeared distressed and anxious over the king's serious condition.

Katherine wasted no time and went straight to the king's bedside, where she sat on a wooden stool placed next to his ornately carved tester bed. She lifted his hand, listless and warm, to her lips and pressed a kiss to his slender fingers. Turning his head, the king opened his eyes to see Katherine, his cherished childhood friend and lady consort, her eyes now brimming with pitying tears.

"Katherine, Katherine, is it really you?"

"Aye, it is I, Katherine. You sent for me, and I have come. I am truly here, my king."

Her voice trembled with emotion. "Oh, Jamie, my king, how is it that you are so ill?" She placed a hand on his forehead and became alarmed at the fever and his obviously grave condition.

The king lifted a hand to her cheek; but his strength failed him, and he dropped his hand to the pillow.

"Surely, this illness cannot be so bad, Jamie. Indeed, you will recover, my lord, as you have in previous times," Katherine insisted.

As his eyes searched her beautiful face, he remembered the years when Katherine was at court and the deep love he had for this tender young girl. He had relentlessly pursued her; but she had refused his advances, so he had issued a royal summons that she could not refuse. In the years that Katherine was at court, they'd had a son together, wee Johnny. Illegitimate though he was, Jamie loved him and would provide for the child's future. He must tell Katherine he was sorry, so terribly sorry.

"Nay, Katherine, it is over. I canna recover. There is too much, too late; and I am sorry, so sorry to take you away . . . from Robbie. Forgive me, Katherine. I am sorry."

"It is never too late, my king. I forgive all that happened in the past. Do not distress yourself over the lost years." She glanced around the room and beckoned for a servant to bring some fresh water. She dipped the cotton cloth in the cool water and bathed the king's face.

"You must try. Try to get well. Be of good courage; be comforted. God is ready to forgive, to help you, to grant you peace." Hot tears streamed down her face as she earnestly pleaded with the king.

Shaking his head from side to side, the king seemed unable to grasp her words of hope. He waved the dampened cloth away. "The battle . . . ye have heard . . . at Solway Moss . . . lost . . . so many died . . . me standard taken, my fault . . . I wasn't there to lead."

"Ye kin, all kings know the fortunes of war are never certain, aye; and good or bad, the results of conflict cannot be foreseen, Jamie.

The battle may be lost at Solway Moss, but Scotland is still here and will survive. Do not despair."

"Pardon me, m'lady," interrupted one of the physicians tapping gently on Katherine's shoulder and speaking softly into her ear. "His Majesty is plagued with a persistent fever, but his unwillingness to fight for his life will not allow him to recover from the illness. His depressed state is causing him to lose the battle. Pleas, if ye can rouse him from his despair, perhaps he will recover."

Understanding the seriousness of his warning, Katherine nodded; and the physician withdrew a discreet distance to allow Katherine privacy.

"Dear Jamie, my old friend," Katherine, still gripping his hand, began in a halting voice, "you are young, only thirty years, and your life is before you. The kingdom needs you. You are Johnny's father; think of your children and fight to live, for their sake, for the kingdom's sake. Oh, do not give up."

The king studied Katherine's face, trying to understand her words.

As Katherine held his hand, listless and hot, the king shook his head in negation. "Katherine," he said, his voice barely audible, "I have loved you . . . and had ye been of royal blood . . . "

"Nay, Jamie, please, do not speak of it. So long ago now and we have moved beyond those difficult days. We have both been wounded, lost in some ways; but we have gained in other ways, so try and remember the good."

"What good, Katherine? Ye be the only good, ye kin? God is punishing me—took my two wee boys, little lads they were, heirs to the kingdom—but God took them because of my wickedness. Aye, the spirits of evil haunt me, torment me in the dark of the night, Katherine."

"Children die of illness—not because of you, not because God is cruel. But remember, a new heir is coming; and you must think that God is blessing, not cursing you. You have other children—healthy children—not heirs, perhaps, but still your own. Aye, Jamie, please, I beg of you, do not allow this despair of past failures to take your hope of recovery."

The king appeared as though he had not heard her words. "Your father, Sir John, once told me . . . words that haunt me, frighten me, plague me. He said"—the king took a shuddering breath—"be a good king, Aye, that's what he said to me; and Katherine, I am not a good king."

"All men make mistakes, my lord, and kings are no exception. Jamie, remember this, you can right the wrongs. Now, please try and rise from this bed and go forward and be a good king."

"Ye know, my sweet lass, that I have taken lands, aye, stolen them from my people, killed many for greed, punished the heretics most cruelly." He sighed deeply. "Aye, Katherine," he said looking into her troubled, earnest face, "I am not a good king."

"But there is forgiveness, for God is ready to pardon and is near to the humble and contrite,"[22] Katherine encouraged the dying monarch. "And 'though your sins be as scarlet,' God will wash them 'as white as snow.'[23] You can be a good king. Remember God's mercy, Jamie. Have faith in his words that promise forgiveness to all who call on Him."[24]

A priest came forward to speak to Katherine. "M'lady, the king has received the last rites, so I request that you not trouble him with words of repentance. The king has received absolution from the pope himself."

---

22   Isaiah 57:15
23   Isaiah 1:18
24   Psalm 86:5

"Then, I beg of you," Katherine said to the priest, her eyes flashing with indignation, "tell the king that! Can you not see that he is not at peace? Are you so blind to his dying needs?"

Waving the priest away, the king turned to Katherine. "Ye heard the priest, Katherine—they have prayed, anointed me, said holy rites, said I am ready—perhaps time in purgatory—but I be absolved of my sins . . . they say. Absolved?" His eyes teared up and moved around the bedchamber as though searching for something.

"Always before me, torturing my mind. Please, Katherine, I beg of you, my true friend, faithful friend, buy masses for me, say prayers . . . " The king's words were growing more disjointed, drifting into silence.

"Do not speak as though you will not recover, my Lord, for thinking dark thoughts will worsen your outcome and hasten your demise. Oh please, Jamie, do not depend on the priest; but as a man with one soul, call on God for forgiveness."

Alarmed and desperate, Katherine leaned close to his ear to whisper. "You must pray for yourself, my king, my old friend. I beg of you, call on the God of Heaven!""

Again, the king shook his head. "Nay, I will not recover," insisted the king, "and will soon . . . leave this world. Last rites offered, sweet lass, anointed with holy oil . . . eternity awaits." His breath became more labored.

"Nay, nay, you must not think so," Katherine said, ever more concerned over the king's deep depression. Her mind swiftly evaluated the king's torment, his obsession with seeing himself as the "bad king" and searched for positive words to raise his spirits from the depths of misery and unbelief.

Katherine pondered the priest's words, advice that felt safe to King James, knowing he would face whatever came next with his sins absolved. He trusted the pope, who had sent word that he would surely be saved in the afterlife. After all, His Holiness, the pope, head of the Mother Church, was, in the king's opinion, trustworthy; and James had followed the dictates of the Romish Church all of his adult life.

A loud rapping at the door of the bedchamber startled the physicians and priests remaining to assist in the death vigil. As the insistent knocking continued, a servant hurried to open the door.

A messenger in the royal livery of Linlithgow Palace handed a message wrapped in heavy vellum to Adam Otterburn, an important servant of the Scottish monarchy. Serving as the king's lawyer, advisor, and trusted diplomat, he was waiting quietly in the shadows of the bedchamber. He opened the missive, looked to the king, and proclaimed in a loud voice to all those gathered in the room, "Queen Marie has been delivered of a healthy babe—a lass, a female heir to the throne. God save the heir of King James V of Scotland!"

"Here, here!" echoed the voices throughout the bedchamber of the king.

On hearing the message, the king immediately attempted to rise from his bed but fell back onto the pillows in a state of weakness and despair. "A lass," he said with obvious disappointment in his tone. "The kingdom came in with a lass, and now it will go out with a lass." The king turned his head away and said no more.

A feeling of dread and foreboding came over the entire company gathered there. Katherine began to weep softly, praying earnestly that the king would yet recover. She remembered the days of their youth and the earnest pleadings of the young, fatherless boy, so wounded, denied the comfort of home and family, held captive by his stepfather, a boy king with burdens too heavy for his young shoulders.

Compassion filled her heart, as well as contempt for the regents who had ruined him and taken advantage of his inexperience and youth, leaving him with a kingdom to rule and a conscious that warred against his very nature. Still, he had so doggedly pursued her, the daughter of a knighted soldier but not of royal blood. She had loved him as a friend, even as a brother; but she could never return his love.

She should hate him, despise him; but he was Johnny's father, a child born to the unwilling union, the only way the king could have her—a consort, a partner, a companion, but never a wife. As Jamie lay dying on his bed, depressed and wordless, all that welled up in Katherine's heart was pity for the wasted years, the guilt, and the shame of a monarchy left without a male heir, only a wee babe, and, if she lived, a girl child who was destined to rule Scotland.

The desperate physicians applied steaming salts and herbs for the king to breathe to rouse the king from his stupor, but he did not revive enough to speak again. He drifted slowly into unconsciousness, his hand falling limply from Katherine's grasp.

He lingered for some hours, despite the efforts of the physicians and priests; but it wasn't long until the young king took one last breath. James V, king of Scotland, age thirty, was dead, leaving his only legitimate heir, a wee babe, only days old, who would one day become Mary, Queen of Scots.

Chapter 27

Surely goodness and mercy shall follow me all the days of my life:
and I will dwell in the house of the Lord forever.

Psalm 23:6

JENNY CHANCELLOR GALLOPED HER DAPPLED pony through the
April sunshine, inhaling the scent of the spring wildflowers dotting
the meadows. Pockets of warm air wafted in the breeze, kissing her
cheeks like ribbons of silk and promising a welcome relief from the
recent harsh Scottish winter.

Today, she would see Peter; and along with other young people
and local crofters, they would make merry after months of winter
separation. They would gather in the lovely region of Tinto Hill, a
promontory rising majestically from the west bank of the River
Clyde. Her waving red hair blew free in the wind as she galloped
toward Tinto Hill. Her cheeks were flushed pink with anticipation.

A picnic and spring frolic, an annual event so loved by the locals,
was planned for the day. Those living in the Clydesdale area of the
southern uplands gathered each spring to celebrate the end of winter,
a time to make merry and to reacquaint with friends and neighbors.

On arriving at the designated area for the picnic, Jenny noticed
Peter talking with his long-time friends, Alistair Eliot, Hamish

Cockborne, Ian Leslie, and Gordy Baird, all covert resistance leaders of the current persecution of the Christian people of Scotland. Jenny feared the recent execution of the popular reformer, George Wishart, would dampen this gathering.

So much had happened in recent months. King James V had died soon after the disastrous battle at Solway Moss. His only heir, a tiny infant girl, Mary, was declared the next ruler of Scotland; but until she came of age, regents ruled the land with Archbishop David Beaton wielding his influence and power over the entire kingdom.

With the tragic martyrdom of George Wishart, heretic trials reached deeper into the border regions of Scotland as Beaton intensified his search for dissenters. After King James had granted a full pardon to William Carmichael, Beaton had set his eyes on the young Scottish Reformer, George Wishart, vowing to hunt him down or lure him to Edinburgh and deceive him on false pretense, only to betray him.

Wishart was an eloquent and dynamic preacher, full of grace and wisdom. He had graduated with honors from King's College in Aberdeen and then studied at the University of Leuven in Belgium. There, he learned of the teachings of Luther and other Christian Reformers preaching the truths of the New Testament gospel and denouncing the false teachings of the pope and the Romish Church.

Another zealot and staunch supporter of Wishart was the young John Knox, who traveled with Wishart, aiding him in his missions and acting as a protector if trouble was threatening. Both were highly educated men who dared to expose the non-biblical pagan teachings of the papal church.

The Protestant Reformation was spreading across Europe, even reaching to the Highlands of Scotland. Times were perilous for those who were protesting the deception of Catholicism. Men like Martin Luther were proclaiming, "The just shall live by faith," his words considered by the Romish Church to be a heretical doctrine. Heresy was punishable by death, and Rome still wielded the balance of power in Scotland.

Despite the dangers, Wishart's following grew. He preached in fields and hidden glens throughout Scotland at the very peril of his life, while Beaton and the royal guard actively hunted him, swearing to put an end to his life. The king was dead, so Beaton could not revoke the pardon for Carmichael; but he could find another Reformer to exact his vengeance.

Jenny waved a friendly greeting to Peter and his group of friends. Seeing Jenny, her auburn hair glistening in the spring sunshine, Peter excused himself from his companions and ran to where Jenny was tethering her horse to a wild cherry tree, giving the mare a long lead to graze in the new spring grass. The couple laughed together in a joyous greeting, clasping both hands together, their eyes shining with pleasure.

"Come, sweet lass," Peter said to Jenny, his delight at seeing her apparent. He drew her a little distance to where several logs were arranged in a semi-circle beneath some ancient oak trees.

"Aye, Jenny, the lads and meself dragged these logs from the forest to use for seating and made these crude tables from scraps of lumber. Will work for our spring festivities, aye?" He smiled broadly, bowing like a prince and then seating Jenny on the rugged log benches.

"Oh, aye," said Jenny, laughing, her eyes sweeping over the gathering of women setting out food and shooing away children trying to poke their fingers into the pies. Excited greetings were exchanged, and laughter echoed throughout the gathering of animated merrymakers.

"Have you heard the amazing details of George Wishart's death, Jenny?" queried Peter. "My friends and I were just discussing how Wishart faced death with faith and courage. Ye kin, Ian Leslie, sitting over there with the other Resistance workers, heard it from a kinsman, Norman Leslie, at Saint Andrews, a man gathering a network of believers determined to stop that wicked cardinal from future executions. And, Jenny, I plan to join them."

"Join them? Those Northern men are noblemen, lairds of vast land holdings and definitely not in our league. So just how are you planning to enlist in such a dangerous undertaking? Are you daft, Peter?" Not waiting for an answer, she continued, "Moreover, Peter, your da' and Sir John will surely object to such a scheme."

Not waiting for an answer, she continued, "Moreover, Peter, your da' and Sir John will surely object to such a scheme. "

"I don't plan to tell them of our plans to rid the country of those wicked evildoers. Besides, for years, Da' has secretly warned covert gatherings of raids on their secret meetings, even rescued some from execution pyres, so I do not feel he would object to such a mission."

"I believe you are wrong, Peter. Warning the believers is one thing, but getting rid of our persecutors by violent means sounds like quite another thing. Sounds like a plot of pure revenge to me."

"Not revenge, Jenny—simple justice. I am not the one planning this bold move, but if the cause is just, and the northern lairds have influence, I want to be a part. I have been waiting for this opportunity for months, even years. After seeing how my own father was so horribly mistreated in his months at the tollbooth, I vowed to do something to aid the cause of justice."

Jenny studied her boots, but she said nothing. A slight shake of her head was all Peter needed to know about her feelings.

"But, ah, sweet lass," said Peter wanting to change the uncomfortable subject, "no more of this heavy talk. Such a beautiful day in bonnie Scotland, and we have come together to make merry on this spring day, aye?"

Jenny offered a small smile, her green eyes softening. Uncertainty was evident in her tone, and she gently squeezed his hands still clad in his worn leather gloves. "I agree to that. No more talk of sad things. But tell me, Peter, are you missing me after our weeks of separation?"

Peter shook his head, and his face reddened. "Sorry, Jenny. I was so caught up in Ian's account of Wishart's trial and death that I forgot my manners. Forgive me, lass; I am a bungling idiot. I have missed you, of course—missed our talks, especially discussing our plans for the future."

Jenny's eyes shadowed with unease, and a secret smile tugged at the corners of her mouth. Sighing, she said, "Oh, my dear Peter, you are such a zealot for truth and the gospel that you do forget everything else, even me."

"Nay, Jenny, do not think it, a thousand times, nay. I see you in every sunset that paints the sky; ye are my heart, my soul, my only love. And someday soon, I promise you, we will be together, even if it means defying your father. Nay, sweet lass, I could never forget you."

"Ye wax poetic, Peter, and I believe you mean what you say; but the reality is that there will always be another wrong to right, another believer to save. I grow weary with the never-ending talk of how Scotland must proceed in this ongoing fight for the faith."

"Aye, Jenny, we fight for truth against an ungodly beastly system of men, and that system is not easily conquered. Already, years have passed; and still, we fight on. Who can say when Scotland will be free of tyranny and from papal rule?"

Turning her gaze to see the young Resistance workers now in animated conversation, Jenny said, "So, Peter, only tell me what you understand from Ian's report, and then we shall not speak of it again today. We have little news that is trustworthy at Shieldhill—only that Wishart was executed as a heretic and traitor. I do want to hear about his death, his last words, his prayer."

"Jenny, love, it is a dreadful account."

"Perhaps, but still, I want to know about his courage, Peter, how he faced death with hope and faith. I'm sure it will encourage me; and, Peter, I need faith."

"Then let me relate to you what Ian has shared with me." Peter sighed heavily. "After the executions of the believers in Glasgow in '39, the council hunted for more victims."

"We heard there were more executions. The news even stretched to Shieldhill; but, Peter, when that news reached our doorstep, my father did not rejoice at this news. I feel he is softening his view of this ongoing search for dissenters."

"Our prayers are being answered on behalf of your father, Jenny. After we caught him reading that forbidden Testament in his own library, I felt God would convict him of the error he has so long supported."

"That has been my prayer, Peter, that God would open his eyes."

"Anyhow, the heretic hunters found six more believers in Perth that they could torture and kill. While preaching the gospel of truth around the Scottish countryside, George Wishart escaped capture many times. Then Archbishop Beaton himself sent a personal invitation, persuading Wishart to come and explain his beliefs in the New Testament gospel without fear of arrest or harm. Wishart trusted them, thinking they were searching for truth."

"And he believed that biased council?" Jenny shook her head in disbelief. "Ye know, Peter, once you are in their hands, they will never honor their word. They are only interested in getting you there to get their hands on you."

"Aye," agreed Peter with a heavy sigh. "John Knox, his helper in all things, tried to warn Wishart. Knox served Wishart, loved him as a godly prophet, said the grace of God was upon him, so full of faith and wisdom. Wishart preached the truth to the Scottish people without fear or favor. But Knox felt uneasy about Wishart accepting an invitation to attend a meeting with Beaton."

"And remember how he cared for the people of Dundee when they were sick and dying from that terrible plague," said Jenny in a low whisper as though she didn't want to awaken painful memories.

"He preached hope and salvation to those suffering people," said Peter, "ministering among the sick without fear. His love for the people won the heart of Dundee."

"I still find it hard to believe that George Wishart, that good and godly man, was so cruelly betrayed and martyred," Jenny said, tears forming in her eyes. "What did you hear from Ian, Peter?"

"Well, Norman Leslie, Ian's kin living in Saint Andrews, says that Wishart traveled to Ormiston to preach. John Knox was with him;

but Wishart forbade him to accompany him, told him to go home and be at peace. On arriving in Ormiston, Wishart had supper with guests at the Lord of Ormiston's home. After supper, Wishart sang a Psalm and went to bed."

"I have heard it said that he had a beautiful singing voice and sang Psalms every night before he retired to rest. Such a comfort in his time of great trouble," Jenny said.

"At midnight," resumed Peter, "Beaton's henchmen surrounded the house, and there was no escape. Then, the Earl of Bothwell, that malicious traitor, took Wishart bound to Edinburgh Castle and later transported him to that despicable sea tower dungeon at Saint Andrews, where so many believers met their death."

Peter looked away into the distance, remembering the betrayal and death of Patrick Hamilton, the execution he was forced to witness. He gazed into Jenny's stricken face; her green eyes welling up with tears.

"Aye, Jenny, Wishart was tried and condemned as a heretic by the church council. He was sentenced to hang and then burned. They feared burning him alive, since he had great influence among the people. They executed him at the west part of the castle near the priory."

Peter felt hot rage rise in his breast. His anger for David Beaton, that murdering cardinal, was quickly growing beyond reason. He wanted to stop this evil man from imprisoning and killing more Christian believers. He vowed to join others who wanted to stop that wicked man at any cost, even if they had to kill him.

"Peter, Peter," Jenny said softly as she laid a gentle hand on his arm. "Do not tell me more. I see that it grieves you, and it makes us both sad. I feel your anger, and I am sorry that it hurts you so much. Let us not allow this unfortunate event to spoil our day together."

"Nay, Jenny, I must finish, painful though it may be." Peter drew a ragged breath; and taking Jenny's hand, he continued.

"The royal guard dragged Wishart to the execution site, where he knelt and prayed; and then he spoke to the crowd waiting for the execution to take place. His words were bold and confident, taken down on parchment by his followers."

Peter paused, his hands fisting with emotion. "Wishart said, 'If I had taught men's doctrine, I had gotten greater thanks by men. But for the true gospel, which was given to me by the grace of God, I suffer this day by men, not sorrowfully, but with a glad heart and mind.'"

"He was so bold, Peter, so brave! Go on. Were those all his words?"

"Nay, lass, his last words are what has inspired me to join the Resistance leaders on their mission to rid the country of Beaton. Wishart said, 'I fear not this fire; and if any persecution comes unto you for the Word's sake, do not fear them that slay the body but have no power to slay the soul.[25] I know surely that my soul shall sup with my Savior tonight.'I memorized his words. It gives me inspiration and hope to remember them."

"What happened next, Peter?"

"Then he prayed for his enemies, for those who had so fiercely persecuted and slandered him. He spoke these words, 'I forgive them with all my heart.' Then they hanged him and burned his body; but as with the martyrdom of Patrick Hamilton eighteen years ago, it rebounded back to the cardinal. Wishart's death has inspired all

---

25   Matthew 10:28

believers, and another fight for Reformation is rising. George Wishart died for the truth, and he did not die in vain."

Laughter drifted from a group of eager young lads setting up straw targets for a contest with spears and bows. They motioned for Peter and Jenny to join them. Reluctantly, the couple joined the group of young people challenged by the horrific events of their day. But always in the hearts of the young, spring brought renewed hope; and once again, they rose to the challenge.

At the edge of the clearing surrounded by various shrubs, trees of birch, pine, and wild cherry, two riders regarded the crowd of happy people tending to pots of steaming venison, pork, and wild turkey, slowly cooking over oakwood bonfires. Some were busy organizing games for the children who were running about playing with wooden swords, young boys chasing the girls amid screams of laughter.

Dismounting Sebastian, his war horse, Sir John Carmichael winked at his brother, William, who offered a rare smile at the enthusiastic gathering. Sir John felt a quickening in his heart, an old familiar reminder of his own times—of his people, his clan, those he loved and cared for, those he wished to protect. Unbidden, tears rose to his eyes.

Sir John Carmichael, chief of the ancient lands of Carmichael and his beloved people, raised his hands to the heavens, quietly beseeching God to spare them from the ravages of inquisition and death, to grant this one day, a time of peace and joy. He could hear the laughter of his nephew, Peter, who had just scored with his bow hitting the target dead center with his own specially crafted arrow.

Laughing, Sir John turned to William. "Your son, my impulsive nephew, is surely in love with Genevieve Chancellor."

"That be certain, John."

"He is young, not yet humbled by life as you and I, William. He has faith and still believes and enjoys life, despite all the opposition. This is good, aye, and speaks of his character. Reminds me of Peter in the Bible. He is aptly named, aye?"

"That be so, John, he is aptly named. His mother named him, handing him to me and saying with her dying breath, 'This be Peter.' Perhaps," William said thoughtfully, "Maggie thought it would be a good name to guide him through life."

William had recovered almost fully from the mistreatment suffered while a prisoner in the tollbooth. Only a slight limp remained from his months of incarceration and rehabilitation. He stood next to Sir John, the two brothers watching the contest from a distance. The young people shouted and laughed as they shared the joy and happiness of this perfect springtime day.

"As we age," Sir John said, speaking from long years of experience, "we grow quiet and reflective and view life from what we have learned about ourselves."

"Aye, is so, John. What once seemed so important during our youth . . . as we grow older, those things seem to fade into the background. What remains are most valuable—love, joy, peace, our lands and home, our family."

William reached for Sebastian's reins and tied the horses to sturdy branches. "In two months, dear brother, I will be a married man. This is reason to rejoice, aye, John?"

"Aye, indeed. A happy day for you and for all our people. Ye are a blessed man to find love again. Your sweet Lorna will brighten the halls of Carmichael House, for certain. And then, if God is willing, Peter will marry Jenny; and once again, the rooms at Carmichael will fill with joy and laughter, aye, William?"

"So true, me brother. We are a household of menfolk; but when I bring my lovely wife home to Carmichael, then Lorna, with all her feminine and winsome ways, will soften our bungling, rough manhood ways, aye?" William smiled broadly. "Lorna makes me feel young again, John, and it is so amazing!"

Sir John Laughed heartily, throwing back his head, his blue eyes sparkling with delight and his stalwart frame shaking with merriment.

"Oh, to be young again! But remember, brother, if we keep in our heart the vision of hope and can see beyond our present difficulties to the beauty of each new day, we will stay young in our heart; and our joy and peace we have in the Lord will never grow old, aye, William?"

Coming Soon . . .
Storm Against the Wall:
Reformation Revealing

Afterword

WRITING HISTORICAL FICTION IS NO easy task, especially a story that involves treachery and deception, good and evil. The notable and factual accounts must be historically correct; and although some events are fictionalized, the characters taken from historic accounts must be convincing, believable, and compelling.

Several times, I visited Scotland, the setting for this series. While visiting my ancestral estate in Lanarkshire, Scottland, I could feel the connection of generations past tugging at my heart, remembering the pathos of those who lived and loved through perilous times. I wanted to write about this time in history, but such a project seemed too daunting.

But when I stood on the very spot in Edinburgh and Saint Andrews, the place where the martyrs were tortured and burned for their faith in the New Testament Reformation gospel, I felt compelled to share their story. I knew that whatever I wrote of those haunting times in history, I could never truly do it justice. I ask my readers to be forgiving as I attempt to share the events that brought to a dark world the light and truth of the everlasting gospel.

We look to the historians who left in ink and blood a written account for this present generation to remember, imagine, and ponder. From the pages of history, their bloody footprints walked and talked through my mind, speaking their story, a time that must not be forgotten, lest we repeat it. From these personal and written historic accounts, I have written my story. Let us remember those who paid the ultimate price to honor God's Divine Word.

From history and my imagination, I, the writer, envision the impacting scenes that happened between the lines, pen those tender and stirring words never recorded in history, remember love known only in secret, and write about the honor and integrity of those whose brave deeds and undying love were never valued or remembered—except by God.

—*Ruth Ann Ellinger, Author*

About the Author

RUTH IS AN AWARD-WINNING AUTHOR of inspirational and historical fiction and nonfiction, twice recipient of American Christian Writers' Writer of the Year award and the Brandon Arts Council's Artist of the Year award for Excellence in the Arts. She is founder and past president of Brandon Christian Writers and co-director of Florida Inspirational Writers Retreat. Ruth is a proud member of the Daughters of the American Revolution and two Scottish clans. She lives in Florida with her retired pastor/husband, Wright. They have four grown children.

For resource references, see book one, *The Broken Spear*

Visit Ruth at www.ruthellinger.com
www.facebook.com/Author.Ruth.Carmichael.Ellinger
www.pinterest.com/AuthorInsights
www.instagram.com/ruthellinger

Also by Ruth Ellinger

The Wildrose Trilogy:
The Wild Rose of Lancaster
Wild Rose of Promise
Sword of the Wild Rose

The Stone of Destiny:
The Broken Spear

Women of the Secret Place: A Collection of Inspirational Stories and
Personal Moments with God

All available through your favorite retailer.

After Catherine Reed's husband dies, she moves back home in order to accept a new position as the teacher for the town's one-room schoolhouse. Samuel Harris has suffered his own loss and guilt has burdened him ever since. When his old flame comes back to town, he wonders if they can find healing together . . .

At the heart of this gripping tale is Orazio, the wayward son of a construction magnate, living a reckless life like that of his artistic hero Caravaggio. He finds himself befriended by Nicolo, the devoted son of a powerful Sicilian mafia clan, who wants to uphold the honor of his family. As the dark underbelly of the art world and the Vatican expose their true character, Orazio finds himself in a world where his loyalty is tested, honor is at stake, and the boundaries between life and art blur.

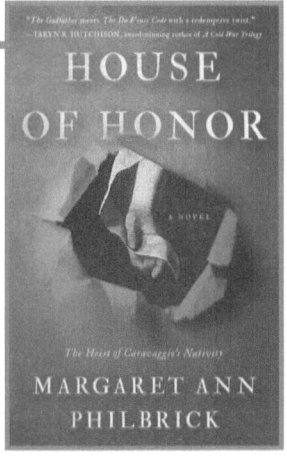

Stevie is a typical teenager of the sixties. But when her dad dies, she and her mom find themselves living a life they never expected. Annie has it all—a loving husband, money, and a beautiful home. But all she has ever wanted is to be a mother. Two women find themselves on two separate journeys to make the greatest sacrifice for the child they love. But can love truly conquer all? Or will the greatest sacrifice be too much?